Dust of the Earth

Dust of the Earth

VERA AND BILL CLEAVER

J. B. LIPPINCOTT COMPANY
Philadelphia and New York

U.S. Library of Congress Cataloging in Publication Data

Cleaver, Vera.
  Dust of the earth.

  SUMMARY: Fourteen-year-old Fern and her family face chal-
lenges and hardships when they move to a farm in South Dakota.
  [1. Family life—Fiction. 2. South Dakota—Fiction] I. Cleaver,
Bill, joint author. II. Title.
PZ7.C57926Du   [Fic]   75-18939
ISBN-0-397-31650-X

FOR DOC AND BERYL

and Theirs, Past, Present & Future

Dust of the Earth

Chapter One

It is my assessment that we are all born to lonesomeness and spend a good deal of our life's time trying either to hide it or to get rid of it. I write of the terribleness of this and other things related, in this, a piece of history of my family. My name is Fern Drawn and in the days of my children my family and I shall probably be thought of as pioneers.

Listen.

I was fourteen years of age and only a passable and not very loyal school student. Offbeat tales of the weird breeds of people of my state of South Dakota which link my pale present with their daring, absurd, dangerous, enviable pasts always interested me more than anything I could get in a schoolroom.

Once I was privileged to stand beside the graves of Martha Jane Canary Burke and James Butler Hickok. These two are buried in the Mt. Moriah cemetery at Deadwood and do not enter this tale except they are a part of the human recollection of the old, brilliant West. Probably you know them by their historical, more colorful names, Calamity Jane and the Prince of Pistoleers, Wild Bill Hickok.

Chronicles of Calamity Jane's role in the making of South Dakota history debate one another. Was she a great, flaming beauty or uglier than a mud fence? Was she a good and virtuous woman who traveled around the country nursing wounded Indian fighters back to health or just another camp follower bum who could outtipple, outcuss and outdraw the best of them? Was Wild Bill really her one true heart's desire? And she his? If so, why did they never marry? These questions may not be appropriate for one such as I to ask. For me it is enough that Calamity did, in fact, exist. And I like to think she truly loved old Wild Bill from the first time she clapped eyes on him until the day he died.

If there can be such a thing as a "fine funeral," reports I have read concerning this event lead me to believe that Wild Bill had one. I gather he was a splendid spectacle lying in his coffin all decked out in a new suit and white shirt, his favorite rifle lying alongside his body. His assassin, a man by the name of Jack McCall, was hanged for his crime at Yankton after a trial by rump court, which is a law council having only odds and ends of its former membership and therefore lacking in authority.

Nobody knows why McCall killed Hickok. I have studied account after account of this affair but have never found any two which completely agree. One has it that it was a revenge killing, that Hickok had murdered McCall's brother. Another has it that Wild Bill insulted Jack during a poker game one time and Jack, being long on memory, never forgot it. Who can say? Historians should be more careful, is my opinion.

What I think happened is this: I think Jack McCall, all whiskeyed up, walked into the saloon where Wild Bill was playing a quiet card game with some of his cronies, was seized with a jealous notion and whipped out his gun, and old Bill received his bullet. Hickok was a six-shooter champion and maybe McCall, prancing around, twirling his gun, only intended to show him up. Since a motive for the killing was never established I think the whole thing was an accident. My opinion of the whole thing is, anytime you put men and whiskey and guns together you have got yourself a festival of asses.

I had a friend who said I had an opinion for everything. He said I would argue with a signpost. His name was Ash Puck Joe and he was a maverick member of the Drifting Goose Band in the Indian Yanktonais Tribe. Not one of your Hollywood motion picture versions of a redskin, he, as well as his wife, was government-mission educated and spoke our language. He was a honyock— a farming homesteader, a successful sheepman with a head for business. He lived in a frame house down the road from us and the last time I saw him was the night he came to our door bearing a kettle of soup. He regretted his wife, six children, parents and grandparents could not come also. Their evening chores kept them home.

Ash Puck suppered with us. We had the soup and biscuits. Ash Puck had a passion for Mama's biscuits. He did not think to tell us the thick, good stew contained dog meat until the meal was nearly finished. I thought my brother Hobson, two years older than I, would collapse. As if he had been shot he leaped from the table, one hand to his forehead, the other to his stomach. "Dog!" he whispered. "There was DOG in that soup?" Hobson always had to dramatize everything.

Refusing to feel the pain of the situation myself I said to him, "Oh, Hob, for the Lord's sake, don't give yourself a nervous rigor over a little thing like this. Dog meat is no different than lamb or cow or hog."

"Ha, ha!" shrieked Madge, our eight-year-old. She had a boil at the time, on her right forearm, to which Mama had applied a drawing medicine called Denver Mud. "Ha, ha. Dog. Oh, that's funny. You are funny, Ash Puck."

"Madge," said Mama, "be quiet." Her breeding would not allow her to put her own bowl aside. She finished what was left in it.

In his high chair Georgie sucked the bowl of his spoon and swiveled his look around as if he knew an intimate secret. He was three and whenever I really looked at him I felt the closeness of mystery. He was charged with cunning, sometimes vicious, little ways. There were times when I could think he hated all of us and was not glad to be one of our members. Maybe he had lived before in some other form and some people like us had hurt him, maybe killed him, and now he was back planning to turn the worm? I think fourteen is the year in life when you begin to ask yourself all kinds of crucial questions and begin the search for the reasons of life.

"Dog," whispered Hobson. "I am white and I ate dog. What will people think?"

I said, "Most people can't, in my opinion, so maybe you have not got much to worry about."

"Smart mouth," said Hobson. "I did not ask for your opinion."

"Some things in life are free, Hobbie."

"Don't call me Hobbie and that is not a request."

"Sorry. I keep forgetting. Some things in life are free, Hobson. Where are you going tonight so dressed up? Over to Maizie's to tell her good-bye?"

"I and my family do not eat dog in anything but soup," commented Ash Puck as if that would justify that matter.

"Of course you don't," said Mama. "We never thought you did."

"That is certainly virtuous information," said Hobson. He was that kind of person always a little on the tormented side of life for one reason or another. Like Mama he had beautiful, deep-set eyes and fine-textured skin. Some people are born to the wrong circumstances and he was one of them. He could scarcely tell a screwdriver from a chisel or a hatchet from an axe and was a little on the niminy-piminy side. I could not imagine him in love with a girl but that was his most current torment. He considered himself to be in love with Maizie Green whose father was superintendent of the sugar beet plant where Papa was employed as an accounting clerk.

For the past several days I had thought Hobson might have suicide on his mind so I said to him, "Hob, Maizie is not so much as you think. She is a liar for one thing. Her hair is not naturally that color, she puts stuff on it to make it yellow. I have seen her bare naked so I know. There. Now that will make it easier for you to tell her good-bye, won't it?"

"I saw her too," lied Madge. "One day I was over to her house with Fern and we both saw her bare naked and it is just like Fern says. Maizie is an awful liar. How come she didn't die from TB last year like she said she was going to? Hob, you had better be glad you will not have to see her again after tonight."

"Ohhhhhh," said Hobson. His fierce, inflamed gaze went from me to Madge and then to Ash Puck's large, patient face. "Dog," he said and lunged from the house. Of such things are our prayers and laughter made.

In a parent-to-parent voice Mama said to Ash Puck, "Children. They are a trial, aren't they?"

"Sure," agreed Ash Puck. None of this had disturbed him. He ate two more buttered biscuits while Mama removed the soup bowls. She insisted on doing the dishes by herself that night. I suspect she scoured and scalded them more than once.

Papa was not present, having taken the train that day to Sturgis to buy a bargain he had heard about—a second-hand car of the early Ford persuasion. We needed it to make our move to Chokecherry which was going to be our new home. That and the money for the car had just been inherited from my grandfather Bacon, Mama's father, a man I had seen but once in my life. After his divorce from Grandmother Bacon, he sent Mama to Kansas City to live with a spouseless aunt and receive her schooling and then he more or less abandoned the western part of the state and moved to the eastern section where he became a man of considerable reputation, active in the affairs of politics and successful in his own business, which was meat packing.

The lawyer who brought us, in person, the news of Grandfather Bacon's death was careful to tell Mama that no one in Chokecherry except herself benefited from his death, that he had left the bulk of his estate to a church in his eastern South Dakota town. I think the people of Chokecherry were less generous in their thinking than the lawmakers of the state, who had passed some pretty liberal divorce laws bringing some quick, if impermanent, prosperity to some of its towns. Anyway the people of Chokecherry lost out upon Grandfather Bacon's death.

As her history has it Grandmother Bacon had an evil temper and was not infatuated with the notion of motherhood. When Mama was five the evil one eloped one watery night with a man who owned a wagon works in Omaha and Mama never saw or heard of her again. Grandfather Bacon was that kind of person who looked upon his noble English ancestry as a personal achievement and viewed those not his social and financial equal as an unbelievable offense. To him we Drawns were the dust of the earth; we were below his salt.

But I am afield now. To come back to Ash Puck Joe and the night of the dog soup. Ash Puck said his good-byes to Mama, Madge and Georgie and he and I walked outside. In twelve hours, sooner if possible, we would be leaving this place. Our rented house and its rented contents had been sold to a family new in the town.

It was the time of the prairie fall with haze, the color of smoke, lying thick on the bright, nibbled hills during the day hours and great flocks of excited, cawing birds streaking south and east, heading for the valleys of the rivers to join others of their kind in mighty, annual migration.

Between daylight and dark there was shooting in the stooks. The wildfowlers were again abroad, as they were every year at this time, hundreds of gunners stalking our ducks and geese and Chinese ring-necked pheasants. In my opinion it was not much of a contest between the hunters and the peaceful birds, it was a nasty, one-sided business. *Boom, boom* sounded the guns and as often as not the birds were not retrieved but left lying where they fell so there was no moral ground for the slaughter.

Papa owned a gun but only took it from its high shelf to clean it. A man of sparse conversation, he had little to say about the hunters. This was cattle and sheep empire so there must have been some land trespassing but still the hunting went on. I might as well tell you we were poor as potato scrapings and could have used some of those unretrieved birds for our own table but Papa and Mama would not allow us to go out into the fields to search among the cornshocks and brush for them. Their reasoning about this being: Better bean-filled stomachs than hunters' targets.

I walked with my friend, Ash Puck Joe, as far as the road. The chill of the evening had come and though the time for bird-singing was mostly past, red crossbills warbled faintly in the starlit grasses. This lover of cone-seeds does not migrate to the south in abundant years. Since they are stingy with their sweet call-songs I thought their presence that night an odd thing.

I thought of something appropriate to say to Ash Puck. "Ash Puck, don't let anybody sell you any wooden nutmegs."

"You darned right," said Ash Puck. He and his brothers and forebears had already been sold enough of the white man's wooden nutmegs to bury the whole state of South Dakota and then some.

After that night I never saw my Indian friend again or heard from him. Maybe he never received the two letters I sent to him and his wife describing our new life at Chokecherry. He was a loyal person and certainly, had my letters reached his hands, he would have made replies. I believed that for the longest while, blaming the mails. Most of us will believe anything to keep from ourselves the knowledge that people, even good friends, are really very separate.

Here I will tell you an interesting fact about the Indians of that time—those that I knew. Their families were usually made up from three generations. Children, parents and grandparents. Each generation had its work. The grandmothers taught the girl children to sew, decorating hide garments with beads, feathers and quills. Grandfathers taught the boy children to fish and hunt for small game. The fathers cared for the stock and quested for peltry and the mothers' work was the cultivation and care of food. Big matters in the families were respect, sympathy and affection. In Ash Puck's family if ever there was any fear of life or death I never saw any show of it and I was close to those people. It was Ash Puck Joe who taught me what I knew about sheep. When we got to Chokecherry we found we had inherited a flock of the woollies.

This is a good place to tell you a peculiar thing about my family. We were not one. There were seldom any announcements of affection between us. We were like partridges in the wood, each scattered to his own interests except during meal and sleep times. We took pleasure in deviling one another. We were not friends— we lived as nuisances to each other, unconfiding, each forever in the way of the others, our ambitions and disappointments forever clashing. The word *love* was not spoken in our house.

It was a dispiriting thing for me to have to say good-bye to Ash Puck that night for it was from this homely man of good will and his family I had learned some things about my own family and myself as well. There was a certain maddening secretness to these and they were weak for they showed me no clear-cut boundary between thinking and feeling. But there would come a day, and soon, when I would see them as a powerful map.

I am not now ashamed to confess to a grubby tear or two as I watched Ash Puck go from my life, yet I could not speak of this sorrow to any one of my family. It was the personal nightmare of each of us Drawns to be judged sentimental.

After my little private storm had passed I went back to the house and helped Mama with more of the packing of those effects which belonged to us and would go with us to Chokecherry. These were rolled in blankets and stashed in containers of every size and description. We roped them to the fenders and running boards of our second-hand car. There was one small, crammed pickle barrel which would ride on the back floorboard. After that night our bedding would be anchored flat to the top of the vehicle and over it Papa would spread our camping tent to serve as a tarpaulin. We did not own the mattresses on the beds in the house we were leaving.

Mama criticized the car to Papa, saying, "It probably will not get us fifty miles down the road. I knew I should have gone with you to buy it. This is no bargain, North. The man who sold you this piece of junk rogued you."

Holding his calm, Papa replied, "I recognize it is no limousine."

"My father would not have wasted his spit on it," said Mama.

"I recognize that also," said Papa. "Unfortunately he was not there to advise me or furnish me with any more money. It was a case of take it or leave it. The man said I could bring it back if you were not pleased with it. Should I take it back? Maybe that would be best. I will tell you again, Jenny, I think this move to Choke-cherry is a mistake for us."

"We have land there and a house, thanks to my father," rebutted Mama. "And that is more than we have here or have ever had anywhere else for that matter. I remember the house."

"I don't see how you could, you were only five when you left there."

"It is made of pink rock that my father brought from Sioux Falls and it has a fireplace made of petrified wood from the Badlands."

"Jenny—"

"It is trimmed in sandstone from Hot Springs. Beautiful. And I remember the bank there, my father started it. It was the first in Chokecherry."

"Fine, fine. Maybe it is still there. Maybe they will let me work in it."

"It is still there, North. I asked the lawyer. He said my father was still remembered at Chokecherry. Why should he not be? He was one of its founders. You will find employment there. I am sure that will be one of the least of our worries. It is too bad, North, you never learned to know my father."

Papa said nothing more. Rebukes from Mama were common in his life, as were comparisons to Grandfather Bacon.

That night my dreams were wild as willy worms. I blamed them on Georgie who had the habit of hogging more than his quota of the bed he shared with Madge and me. I asked him to put his legs together and keep his rump out of my stomach and that little urchin's answer was to deliver a blow with his foot to one of my kidneys. "Tomorrow," I said to him, "you are going to get it from me. I am going to feed you to a coyote."

He laughed. How many times had he heard that promise? He smoothed his nightshirt over his belly and returned to his sleep, legs spread wide, his rump pushed against my stomach.

In the silent, nipping darkness Madge spoke. "And to think," she said, "Mama is going to have another one. Did you know that, Fern?"

"No," I replied.

She said, "Lummox. You never know anything," and pulled her corner of the blanket up over her head and grunted herself to sleep.

The moon laid light across the bared windows and in my restless head I saw Chokecherry, our home there, the first we had ever owned. I did not see our life there as the frontier it would turn out to be, terrifying at its meanest, fascinating and desirable at its best. At Choke-cherry we learned our meanings.

Chapter Two

At dawnbreak the next morning we sat in our car ready to pull out for Chokecherry. It was our intention to follow a southern route to the appropriate turn and then head east. The rogue at Sturgis who had sold Papa our car had given him a road map, but in all the giddiness and twitter of the last minute leave-taking it had become lost.

"Never mind," said Papa. "NEVER MIND. I had a short chance to study it yesterday and there will be signs along the way." There was excitement in his whole figure now that the time to go had come but he was holding it in check.

"Maybe when we stop to refuel we can get another one," suggested Mama. "I don't understand how we could lose such an important thing though."

"Oh," said Hobson, "it's just like everything else we do. Wrong." He gave the collar and cuffs of his light-weight lumber jacket several quick snatches.

Sullen in her share of the back seat Madge said, "The last time I saw it Georgie had it. He was eating it."

Mama jerked her head around to stare. "Oh, in the name of common sense, he could not eat a whole road map. Why didn't you stop him? Does it not ever occur to you, Madge, to correct your little brother when you see him doing something wrong?"

"Yes," said Madge, holding onto her conceit. "But I have found out if I don't do it the way you would then I am the one in trouble."

Georgie was busily adjusting his wool stocking cap with his mittened hands. He pulled the cap down until it covered his ears and eyebrows and said not a word. His eyes, the color of dark raisins, brimmed a dove's innocence.

"He ate the whole thing," said Madge. "I watched him. I told him he had better not. I told him we needed it to get to Chokecherry with. I told him it would make you and Papa mad if he ate it but he didn't pay any attention to me. He hit me on my boil and it hurt. Well, I am through with him. He is not my responsibility."

Georgie sternly and absently decided to clear the matter. "I did not eat any map. I just chewed it up and spit it out." He was a smart little tyke, especially when roused to boredom. He could count to ten and identify all the colors.

"This barrel is in my way," complained Hobson. "There's no place for my feet." It was cold. We had eaten a cold breakfast of hard-boiled eggs and bread spread with colorless oleomargarine and everybody was in foul humor.

To Madge Mama said, "You are becoming too fond of that responsibility excuse. I do not want to hear it come out of your mouth again, you understand?" She turned to Papa and in a testy voice said, "North, can you get us out to the highway without a map?"

"I told you I could," replied Papa. He made no move to start the car. "I TOLD YOU I CAN GET US TO CHOKE-CHERRY WITHOUT A MAP."

"When you talk and look like that you remind me exactly of your father," commented Mama. "I hope you do not have it in your mind to stop off and visit him. If you do, let me remind you now that it will be at least fifty miles out of our way."

"Do you think I want to see him dead?" rebutted Papa. "The last time we visited my folks we almost killed them. I never told you this, Jenny, but the last time we visited my parents they practically asked me never to bring you and the kids back, so the next time I see them I'll go alone."

"That is a relief to my mind," said Mama. She and my grandparents Drawn did not get on well. Grandpa Drawn was a country doctor who carried on his practice in two rooms of his house. He had a surplus of steely beliefs in his own abilities, scoffed at the notion God might be his working partner. He owned books containing knowledge on every scientific subject imaginable but owned no Bible and would not allow table prayer in his home. Grandma Drawn did not enjoy the company of anyone younger than herself and went around with her mouth turned inside out. To be in the presence of those two was to have something drain away from your own.

Papa and Mama had decided not to have words. Papa was saying, "Well, all right now, I guess we can get going." He made several attempts to start the car. It would not start.

Papa said, "Hob, I think the battery in this thing is dead. It's not going to start without some cranking. Give me a hand there."

Hobson groaned, flung himself from the car and went around to the front of it. He and Papa had a little trouble but on the fourth crank the engine fired up. Papa had not yet mastered the art of controlling the vehicle's speed, so we shot out of the yard, down the lane and out onto the road that took us through and out of town faster than he intended, I think. He scoffed at Mama's objection, saying, "Oh, stop worrying. My father taught me how to drive when I was thirteen. I just wanted to show you this car has got guts, that's all."

The high autumn was on us: that calm, counterfeit time between finished summer and winter-nearness when the days give up their seasonal roots and drift in a wasteful, hazy way. The first serious frost of the season had occurred during the night, whitening the ground and trees and grasses. When we went past Ash Puck Joe's place, almost hidden from roadview by a stand of hackberry trees, I saw his house all lighted up. I imagined the movements in it, the children rushing with their chores and breakfast, fearful they would be late for school. They had a long walk ahead of them and there would not be any whining about this. During my close association with them I never heard any whining from any member of Ash Puck Joe's family. They did not fight with or devil one another. They were united.

What unites a family?

Blood, dimwit.

Yes, but something else too.

Language.

If that is so then there is something wrong with ours. It is not right for us. There is something missing from it, something left over from it after we have finished talking—something lost.

On plan we first went south, running along mile on mile over long, monotonous roads. We passed through a couple of little ink-spot towns and then went across a wide belt of gumbo. This is black, fine-grained, silty soil that would substitute for the most obstinate glue made when it turns to thick, soapy, waxy mud after rain. When dry it is powdery and wrinkled and asphalt smooth.

After the gumbo we came out into a valley where there were tree-sequestered farmsteads, some with roadside stands offering fall harvest for sale. Their tenders waved to us. As if wired to the ground wildflowers stood stiff and brown beside the draws and sloughs. There was thistle fluff in the wind and great haystacks in the fields.

The roominess of this land is what impresses the eastern traveler. Our fine, clear air deceives. What appears to be only yards away can be miles distant. I can think that the America-conscious traveler is awed by his first glimpse of the Hills, the Black Hills, the first of the western mountains. They are deep blue, they are purple, they appear black. It is the trees, the dark junipers and cedars of the foothills and, farther up on the slopes, the forests of spruce, ponderosa, lodgepole and limber pine that give the Hills their name.

At the point where we should have turned east we missed, without any of us noticing, and entered a canyon, our road following an old washed-out and deserted right-of-way, modest and open in its beginning but dipping to steeper proportions as we went farther into its depths. The rimrock of this gorge was made up of varying colors and materials: white, red, gray and pale green. Shale, limestone and sandstone. Its rock walls rose on either side to severe heights bringing to mind an embattlement. The sun, moving toward its highest daytime peak, lighted this great earth fracture and its colors swam together. We saw a fall of white, frothy water and heard the wild callings of some kind of canyon birds. I wondered if this place was their permanent home or if they were lost. Papa drove with caution and it was a queer thing we did not meet other travelers.

Madge offered a crafty explanation for this. "They've all gone home so their kids can go to school. Maybe we won't have to go any more this year. Maybe the school at Chokecherry will be all filled up by the time we get there."

"It won't be," promised Mama. To Papa she remarked, "North, I don't believe we should be in here. It seems to me we are going south and not east. Shouldn't we have turned back there? I didn't see any sign, but I have the feeling we should have."

"I missed my turn," said Papa. "As soon as we come to a place where I can turn around we'll stop and have our dinner, then we'll turn around and go back."

Madge and Georgie were sleeping. Hobson was pandering to his suffering over Maizie Green and also he had wrenched his shoulder a little while cranking the car. He had not eaten since Ash Puck Joe's dog soup. I thought it might be his intention to starve himself to death. He sat with his head back and his eyes closed and more than ever looked to me out of place with our circumstances.

In the bottom of this canyon we were in there was a creek. Its banks were amass with brilliant fall foliage and I thought Hobson should be enjoying this scenery. In an instant of limited pity I decided to help him. "Hob?"

He opened his eyes and looked at me, staring into my face as if he expected to see something jump out of it. "What?"

"Hob, I never saw Maizie Green naked."

Hobson's smile was faint and decided. "I know you didn't. I know what a big liar you are, Fern."

"I am no liar, buckaroo. When's the last time you heard me tell a lie?"

"You told Maizie's mother and father you were adopted."

"Oh, sweetest God, that was years ago."

"One year ago. We haven't known them any longer than that."

"All right, one year ago. I was just a kid then and didn't know any better. Now I'm a lady."

"You are no lady, Fern."

"You don't see me as one? Why?"

"You smell loud."

"I?"

"Loud. Your hair stinks. You stink. Can't you smell yourself? Don't you ever look at yourself in a mirror?"

"When I have time I do. I don't see how I can stink. I wash every day, especially my feet. Not my hair of course. I only do that every ten days. You think I want to be bald?"

"You smell like sheep and sheepdog and Indian."

"Well, there is nothing wrong with those odors. There are some people who like them."

"You won't ever find a rich man who does."

"Well, rich men or poor men are nothing in my young life. I am not studying either kind."

"You sure change your mind a lot. Aren't you the

one always saying the first rich man comes along and offers to marry you you'll take him up on it?"

"Oh. Well, yes, that is my intention. He'll have to have some life in his mind though to go along with his money. I think. Money is sure a nice thing to have. Listen, buckaroo, want me to carol you a little roundelay? It will cheer you up and help pass the time."

"You think you're pretty cute in that cowboy outfit, don't you?"

"This is not a cowboy outfit, buckaroo. These are special pants and this is a special jacket made out of pure, cured buckskin. Ash Puck Joe's wife made them for me. Look at all this fancy beadwork, and these are real porcupine quills."

"They smell worse than dead buzzards," stated Hobson in a detached voice and drew into his corner. There might have been more to that conversation but just at that moment we had a blowout. The sound this accident made rang throughout the canyon like a shot from a high-powered gun. We had run over a sharp rock in our road doing severe injury to one of our rear tires.

We did a bad day's work that day. We did not get out of that canyon until nearly duskfall. When the blowout occurred we all got out of the car and stood in the road surveying the situation. Before Papa could open his mouth to ask Hobson for his help Hobson said to him, "I hope you won't need my help with this, Papa. My shoulder is wrenched."

"I am sure sorry to hear that," said Papa looking at

Hobson as if he beheld an alien. Seeing the look, Mama gave Papa a hard one of her own and then instructed Hobson to mind Georgie. She and Madge took our basket dinner from the car and walked down the road a way to choose a pleasant picnic spot, one that the sun reached, leaving Papa and me to cope with our accident.

Hobson lifted the baby from the car and set him on the ground. He tried to take Georgie by the hand but the child was drunk with this new bonus of freedom. Whirling away from Hobson he ran across the road and hurled himself from its edge, his arms outspread like bird wings.

"Good Lord God," shouted Papa and he and I ran across the road too, certain we would see Georgie lying dead at the bottom of the canyon, but he had landed on a piece of slope thick with slick, yellow leaves. He rolled over and over in them, laughing and throwing the leaves into the air. Hobson leaped from the road himself, aiming his body in the general direction of Georgie's leaf pile, but that little dickens was too quick for him. He was on his feet again running away from Hobson zigzag through a stand of quaking aspen trees. Hobson took out after him and Papa and I returned to our trouble. We had never before owned a car so neither of us knew anything about changing a tire. Papa said he could not remember ever having watched his father coping with a blowout. For us then it was a thorny job and there was some danger involved as the roadbed was strewn with small white boulders.

When jacked our vehicle listed a little and I said,

"If this flivver should fall over on us we would both be smashed flatter than flapjacks. Then what?"

"Oh," predicted Papa, "your Mama would manage. She's very capable." His voice had an edge to it and that was his kind of humor and it was a jolt, the estimate of him that came to me then. It had not happened before.

The rays of the sun were white on the walls of the chasm and I thought, for the first time in my life, these wondering things of my father: How is it I have lived fourteen years with him yet never given any attention to the measuring of him? I don't know him nor does he know me and how is that? We have never talked about anything important. He doesn't know what matters to me. What matters to him? His work? No, he hates that. He hated it in Wyoming and then in Nebraska and then in this last place. Does he like me? He has never said. He does not like Hobson. Hobson is Mama's. It is going to take something besides a Maizie Green to make a man of Hobson.

How hard it is to rid yourself of the habit of self-armor even for a minute. Why do we coat ourselves with it? Do we all live a secret life away from the eyes of those who watch us and the ears that hear us?

Squatted in the rough road, working shoulder to shoulder with Papa to replace the injured tire with the spare one which had been riding on one of the front fenders, I said to him, "That old bullwhacker-ghost Grandpa Bacon sure did not do us any favor leaving Mama the money for this jitney. Do you think it will get us to Chokecherry in one piece?"

"I wouldn't bet on it either way," said Papa. "Hand me that wrench, will you, Fern?"

"I never thought he was so much, did you?"

"Who?"

"Grandpa Bacon."

"Oh, he was all right. A little loose in the slats when it came to his money and who he thought he was, maybe, but otherwise I guess he wasn't so bad."

"He hated your guts, didn't he?"

"I think so."

"Why?"

"I never found out for certain."

"Because he didn't want Mama to marry you. But he didn't want her. He sent her away when she was just a little kid. I never thought he liked her very much either. All those long letters she used to write to him but he only wrote to her once a year. At Christmastime."

"Your Mama," said Papa, "is the image of your grandmother Bacon. You should have noticed that, you've seen her pictures. There now, that's the last of the bolts. I hope the jack will hold."

The jack held. In a few minutes the job was done and we walked on down the road to join the others. Mama had spread a cloth on a flat rock and laid out food. Papa and I cleaned our dirt-stained hands on some clumps of grass, then Papa walked back to the car for our container of drinking water. We heard him calling to Hobson. "Hob! Dinner! You and Georgie come on now, we haven't got all day."

Hobson did not answer, he and Georgie did not appear. Imagine our worry. A half hour went by while we waited. Then I went in one direction and Papa and Mama went in two others leaving Madge to sit in the car with instructions to blow the horn at frequent intervals, to blow four long blasts if Hobson and Georgie returned to the car while we were out searching for them.

I was afraid, as all of us were, for at that time this was a brooding, primitive land, a fitting place for wild-prowler animals as well as cutthroats, thieves, murderers and other outlaws. Yet I composed a couple of evil speeches to deliver to Hobson as I clawed my way through brambles of wild plum, buffalo berry and other brush, climbed rock to stare down into ravines, slid down rock studded with rock to look into the openings of little side canyons. There were trails, some appearing to have been frequented, some leading downward to streams or open meadow, others to nowhere.

The sun darkened and then disappeared altogether. The temperature began to drop, the wind stilled, a line of flat, gray clouds formed over the canyon and hung there. Presently they began to release snow, dusting the tops of the canyon rim and all the crags and spires of the higher landscape. Some of the stuff sifted to the ground but melted almost as fast as it hit. In the deep fastness of the deepening cold I heard a sound I remembered from another time in my life in another wild place—the low, coarse bellowing and the clear, high-toned bugling of the wapiti. Autumn is the mating season for the great bull elk.

When four long blasts from the car horn rent the air I can tell you I returned to it and the others with great speed. I was chilled to my marrow. We all were and we were all mad except Georgie who had enjoyed this mischief outing. He had a trophy tucked inside his stocking cap but did not let us see it at once. He held it with both hands, pinching the ends of the cap together so that the bulk of what was inside remained hidden. Dreamy and serene he gave us his side of the escapade. "I didn't do nothing bad. I was a good boy. I only ran away. Didn't you know I'd come back like I always do? I went in a hole and then Hobbie found me and then it snowed a little bit and then Hobbie went to sleep and then I found this." His smile brushed us all.

Mama had got Hobson a wool scarf from a box in the car and he was arranging it around his neck, tucking in the ends of it inside the collar of his lumber jacket. He was still refusing food. His expression was full of a dozen indignations. As if explaining something to us we should already know he said, "I did not go to sleep in any hole. I only laid down a minute to rest. We were not in any hole, it was an old miner's tunnel. Georgie ran in there and I went in after him but couldn't make him come out. I couldn't carry him out. Any of you ever tried to pick him up when he doesn't want to be picked up? You see this eye? Is it turning black? He hit me. He's crazy and ought to be kept in a cage. Look at him, filthy little beast. You know what's in that cap? A skull. A HUMAN SKULL WITH BULLET HOLES IN IT. LOOK AT IT."

Loving his trophy, treasuring it, Georgie released

his hold of the cap. Sure enough it contained a bleached human skull with two round holes in it the size bullets would have made.

Papa said, "That might have some historical value," but before he could do any more examining or stop Mama, she snatched both the skull and cap up, ran to the side of the road and hurled both. The cap did not go far. We heard the clatter the skull made against rocks. Papa went after the cap.

Georgie didn't protest. His calm, clear gaze said to Mama, *I'll get even with you for that. Watch out.* Mama scrubbed his hands with her handkerchief.

The clouds over the canyon were beginning to move southward and the wind shifted; the temperature rose a fraction or two. We were able to get out of that place before darkness fell. We slept beside a road that night in our tent.

Just before we turned in Madge's boil broke. What a foul mess. While Papa and Mama tended it by lantern-light I went outside and saw what I am sure was an aurora. An early moon was above the Hills and the stars were out and, looking to the north, I saw a quivering arc appear, stretching from left to right down to the horizon line, great bands of color, red on the lower border, yellow-green above the red. One minute there would only be three or four of the flaming, fluted streamers and the next there would be ten or twelve.

In his nightclothes Hobson came from the tent and stood apart from me. He was still distrait over the afternoon's experience, over the loss of Maizie Green, over everything. I thought: Here we are, brother and sister, yet I'll bet if I kept count of all the nice words we have said to each other they would not total a hundred. Is that my fault? It is sure somebody's. I said to him, "Look. Oh, look, Hob, before it goes. I think that's an aurora. Look!"

He looked and was uninterested and I wondered then what it would take to shake him out of himself. A man would not look at such a spectacle and look away unimpressed. That is the behavior of a spoiled boy. Or a troubled one.

Chapter Three

I am hard put to it to describe the Badlands of South Dakota, their many-colored soils, their spirit shapes. They crowd impressions of God. They bring to my mind a picture of an old, lost, royal city I have never seen. Covering an east-west stretch of about two thousand square miles in southwestern South Dakota, created not by man or wind but by cloudburst waterwear and water seeping into the porous rocks, washing, washing them, remolding their patterns and shapes, this outlandish landscape is freakish, sense-tricking, a terrible sight and grand. Out of poorly cemented bedrock there have been created spires and columns and peaks standing together and apart. There are humpbacked ridges and flat-topped buttes separated by box canyons; deep, barren gullies and sawtooth divides. On the grassy tablelands and in the low areas of this region there is scant plant and animal life. In winter devil-blizzards send their fury through this desolation. In kinder weather months it shows its colors—green, purple, gold-white. The coyotes howl at night in the awful, raw stillness. Our town of Chokecherry lies to the south and somewhat to the east of this land.

We came to it in midmorning of a Saturday and at first I thought it was pure waddy but after a good look at its two main streets saw that it had its share of farmers, white-collared men and Indians. The Indians looked well behaved going about their affairs. A waddy is a cowhand.

The air was harsh and dry and the wind lifted up little dust twisters, spinning them away to alleys and storefront doorways. Papa parked our car in front of a newspaper office and he and Mama got out and went in to ask directions to our new home. There were a couple of horses standing at the curb with their reins draped around their necks and a man with a foolish look on his face came sailing out of a saloon, leaped aboard one of them and galloped off.

Madge jerked up straight to watch this antic. Her eyes were bright as new nails. We were all filthy and smelled like goats; she was the filthiest and smelliest.

"Haw," she said. "Haw. Now that is something I wish I could do. I wish I could have a horse."

I said, "Wish for a gold mine, you'll get it just as quick."

"I don't know why we always have to be so poor. I wish you would hurry up and get married and get out, then there'd be more for the rest of us."

"True. But don't rush me, kid."

"You're fourteen now, that's old enough. Of course anybody who'd ask you to marry him now would have to be blind. Or desperate."

"Desperate? Blind?"

"Why don't you ever comb your hair?"

"I do. I comb it every morning."

"And why don't you do something about your nose?"

"What is wrong with my nose?"

"It's too round on the end."

"Maybe you'd like me to chop part of it off."

"I wanta get out," said Georgie and he unlatched the front door of the car and sat on the ground grinning at any passerby who would grin back.

Hobson had wasted enough of his eyesight on the town. "What a dump," he commented, his expression pained as that of a dog who realizes he has just swallowed a peach seed. He said his throat was sore, pulled his scarf up around to cover his mouth, closed his eyes and put his head back.

Through the window of the newspaper office I could

see Mama and Papa standing at a counter having a caucus with a man wearing a green-visored cap. He was giving more of his attention to Mama than to Papa. She was as travel-soiled as the rest of us yet managed, as she always did, to look like a lady who knew she was somebody. Her pregnancy, if that was not one of Madge's fabrications, had not yet begun to show. Probably it was not a fabrication since Madge was an expert prier. If it was going to be as it had been with Georgie we would not be told about the coming squalling one until his first scream revealed him. Mama belonged to that class of ladies who could not even discuss with a child the mystery of the belly button.

Followed by Green Visor, Mama and Papa presently came back out to the street and walked over to where we waited. Green Visor looked down at Georgie and said, "Handsome little tyke." And of Hobson he said to Mama, "Uncanny. There sits your father all over again. I still can't believe he's gone. He looked to be in his prime last time I saw him. A fine man, Christian in every respect. One of our schools here is named after him but of course you know that."

"No," replied Mama, "he never told me."

"Well," said Green Visor while Papa regarded him as if he was some kind of human new to him, "he was a modest man."

Papa lifted Georgie back into the car. Green Visor said "Howdy" to Madge and me and proceeded to point out the location of the bank, the courthouse, feed stores, food markets and other places of business. Papa held a square of paper on which Green Visor had drawn a little crude map showing Mama's inheritance of land and home to be at least six miles south of the town.

Madge said, "COUNTRY. AGAIN. And you SAID it was in town. Didn't you say it was in town, Mama?"

For a minute I thought Papa would backhand Madge. He said, "Yes, your mother said the place was in town but she was mistaken. You ever been mistaken? Can you remember back to the time when you were five years old? No? Sit down then and shut your trap. I'm sick of your bellyaching."

It was one of the few times I had seen Mama allow Papa to champion her; usually she turned his gallantry aside. In some way unfathomable to me I think it satisfied something in her to do this. Now again, as on the road in the canyon while I helped Papa change the blown-out tire, the measuring of another physically close to me took place severely and intently.

That Mama was lonely for people more like herself than Papa and Madge, Hobson, Georgie and I came to me in a bewildered flow of feeling. She lived with us and worked for us. Once when we lived in Wyoming she ironed clothes and did baking for the more prosperous families of the town and cleaned the Presbyterian church every Saturday afternoon for a dollar. She taught us, when time allowed and we were willing to sit and listen. She listened to our talk, settled our bickerings and our fights, yet between us and her there was nothing of that silent presence that puts persons in real touch with one another. She and Papa quarreled often, especially at night, behind their closed door they quarreled, yet there was another baby coming. What kept them together, nothing realized from their marriage, nothing gained? Except children. Lodestones.

Following Green Visor's map we took a graveled road out of Chokecherry beelining it over swells in the rolling, blowing plain broken here and there by streams which looked to be permanent and of good quality. Cut and crisscrossed by these watercourses the plain fell toward a valley where bushes grew thick around waterholes. Grayed old tumbleweeds of another season bounced and rolled in the grassed meadows like brittle balloons. It was not yet time for the new crop of these globe-shaped plants to break free of their weak soil moorings and begin their wanderings. This might not happen until the final days of autumn or the first days of winter or when a storm occurred.

Riding our high road we saw the shine of a creek in the eastern distance and turned toward this, following a dirt road, jouncing through boulder fields, through growths of pine timber, cedar thicket, small oaks, groves of box elder, cottonwood and ash, most of these big and thick enough to furnish fuel, lumber and fence material.

Through all of this we descended until there before us lay the full vision of a narrow valley sheltered by hill slopes. Our valley. Our hills. This was it. Home. A permanent one. Finally.

Its outside walls were stone which had been pink at one time, now were smutched with age and weather-grime. It had a fireplace with hearth and mantel con-

structed of Badlands petrified wood. There was an outfitted bathroom and a large kitchen equipped with a
black iron cooking range, a fresh water system in fair
working order and some other somewhat shaky house-
holder comforts. There were five other rooms crowded
with pompous furniture and a dark, earthy-smelling cellar. A glassed-over ferrotype of Grandfather Bacon hung
in an oval frame on the largest wall in the most front
room. The face in this positive unwelcoming photograph
looked down upon us smiling silky scorn. Nobody said
the wall would look better without it. How had anything
so common as death dared overtake this one?

There were two dead rats in the fireplace and Papa
picked them up by their tails and pitched them out the
door. The whole place was odorous and dirty.

A flock of sheep, a corral and shed for them, a hip-
roofed barn and one other outbuilding, a saddle horse
named Ned, two workhorses and a pair of goats were
parts of Mama's inheritance which Grandpa Bacon's
lawyer had neglected to mention.

Also there was Nell Parrott, an ex-tragedienne from
San Francisco, an ex–gold prospector from the Black
Hills, an ex–professional faro dealer from everywhere, an
ex–coryphée from all around, an ex–United States detective and, finally, widow of a murdered rancher from the
county adjoining ours. Faro is a banking game where
players place bets on special layouts, betting on which
cards will be winners or losers as they draw from the
dealing box. A coryphée is a chorus girl.

Coming down from the hill slopes, headed for our

corral, Nell and the sheep and the dog whose name was Clyde appeared about four o'clock. Although from time to time the dog looked to Nell for instructing hand signals he seemed to be more in charge than she, running ahead to check the sheep when they turned in the wrong direction, racing back to remind a laggard he had had enough to eat that day. There must have been seventy-five or eighty of the woollies.

Nell had been in the employ of Grandpa Bacon's lawyer for only a short time. She said she thought the sheep had been one of Grandpa's money flyers. "But I think he was sorry about it the hour it was done. My house is about three miles down the valley from this one, just over the county line, and he came riding down one afternoon offering to sell me the animals cheap. He was disgusted because the herders he hired only stayed till payday. Mr. Bacon was not an easy one to get along with. I told him I did not want the sheep, that I was through with any kind of ranching. There was a man named Ward Driscoll robbed my husband of our savings and then killed him without any reason and that finished me off in this neck of the woods. I don't even own any livestock anymore and have got my place up for sale. The minute I get a bona fide buyer I'm gone."

From the provender we had brought with us plus milk from our doe goat Mama and I prepared an early supper and Nell took the meal with us. She was one of those women with two sides to her. You could imagine her all decked out in soft fluff and furbelows having herself a gay, man-attended time on a Saturday night in some music-dinned place of entertainment and you could see her as one of those hardy little women still in the scenes of the West. A gold prospector working a mining claim from suntime to moontime in some cold gulch in the Hills. A fighter for her own rights as well as those of her neighbors, agile as a gazelle, quick with her tongue and just as quick with her firearms. Maybe a shotgun rider freighting through the black night through the Hills or out across the quivering prairie, her gun lying in readiness across her knees. She was not hard to look at even in her masculine ranch apparel. I judged her to be about thirty-eight or forty.

Helping herself to fried potatoes she said, "I reminded Mr. Bacon there were two good sides to sheep raising. There are the lambs and there is the wool. But he wasn't much interested. I always had the idea he didn't like this place much. He kept it rented and once in a while when he was in this part of the state would come out and look around. You can see what his tenants did to the place. The last ones walked off with all his goats but the two you see out there. I don't know how much you know about goats. Better enjoy this milk while you can. I think your doe is about due to go dry and she won't freshen again until about December when she'll kid again. Do you think you'll keep the sheep?"

"Oh, yes, of course," replied Mama. "We don't know anything about them but we can learn. Other people have."

"You have got the beginning of a good farm flock here," commented Nell.

"Yes," agreed Papa. It was one of his principles not to show a stranger any ignorance if it could be avoided.

Nell said, "Mr. Drawn, there are farm flocks and there are range flocks. Yours is a farm flock. You can take them out every day to feed and water and bring them home again every night. A range flock stays out on the range and the herder stays with it. There's a herder wagon out in the barn good as the day it was delivered. If I am not mistaken Mr. Bacon told me he had it custom made. It's never been used. Don't ask me why one of his tenants didn't run off with that too."

Papa switched the subject. "Was the man who killed your husband caught and brought to justice?"

Nell put a hand over her heart, her face was composed. "No, the state was spared the expense of that. Ward Driscoll was an evil man and deserved hanging. My husband was not the first of his victims. There was a warrant out for him in Montana for killing a Mexican man and another in Nebraska for horse-dragging a woman to her death. Human life did not mean much to Ward, not even his own. During a bad blizzard we had right after he murdered my husband he did away with himself in a coulee down below my place. Put five bullets in his head. The sheriff from Chokecherry said it was the strangest case of suicide he had ever seen. The money he stole from my husband was recovered, all but ten dollars."

"Had I been there I would have had to second the sheriff's opinion," said Papa. "To put five bullets in your own head, now that takes some doing."

For dessert we had stewed dried prunes. Hobson ate one and again complained of this throat being sore. He looked feverish. Mama ordered him to bed.

Nell said she had been riding Ned, the saddle horse, home every night and then back again the next morning. Said Grandpa's lawyer had paid her to stay on until the first of the month which was two weeks away and did Mama and Papa want her to carry out that end of her bargain with him?

Papa said yes and we all left the table to walk outside with Nell. The sheep, so dirty and greasy that instead of being white were all shades of gray, had bedded themselves down for the night. A rain bath would turn them the color of rich cream but Nell said there had been no rain for over a month.

The sheep shelter was a shed, set against the barn, about one hundred by thirty feet with an adjoining corral. Both these protections were surrounded by high board fencing and around the boards there was stretched a mesh wire fence. Nell said the architect of this arrangement had only done half a job, that the board fence was poorly constructed. "And he forgot the grain troughs and feed racks," she said. "Come deep snow you'll have to feed them here, you won't be able to take them out." Papa agreed with all Nell's criticisms.

There was a hunter's moon, not yet fully lighted, and the smell of a coming frost. Mama and Nell talked about the school Hobson, Madge and I would attend. Nell mentioned a rural school which was in operation three miles distant from our place. Mama said she wanted us to attend the school in town, the one named after Grandfather Bacon. Nell said she thought that might prove to be a problem, that the school authorities might not authorize transportation for us.

Mama said, "Oh, of course they will authorize it. My father was one of the founders of Chokecherry, they cannot overlook that."

The strengthening light of the moon lighted the crests of the hemming hills, rested on the forms of the sheep asleep in their corral and the cupola atop our house.

Carrying a lantern, Madge and Georgie had gone into the barn to look at the horses, Mama and Nell following them, leaving Papa and me standing beside the sheep fence. For a reason imperfectly understood I wanted to hear him say something meaningful about this new life we had come into. I wanted to read what was in his face but could not, the moonlight was not bright enough yet. I said to him, "You ever seen a newborn lamb, Papa?"

"No," he replied.

"Sometimes it's orange. I learned that when I helped Ash Puck Joe with his lambing last spring. Of course it doesn't stay that color. Pretty soon it turns white."

"Is that so?"

"Papa, are we going to stay here?"

"Your mother says so."

"What do you say?"

"I say the house there is old and is going to take a

lot of fixing up and that is going to take a lot of money and work."

"Are you going to work at the bank in town?"

"If they will have me. I'll work somewhere."

"How much land do we own now?"

"A little over six hundred acres."

"That is a lot. Why don't we sell some of it?"

"Who to? Nobody's buying land now. Nobody has any money. The man at the newspaper office told your mama and me that Chokecherry had lost five families during the last month. People aren't coming here to live. They're moving away."

"Well, the land still looks good, doesn't it?"

Came then his answer which to me was unsettling. It was that way because in his voice there was desire for the land. He had never owned any. He was the son of a physician and yet he had never owned anything except several boxes of books. I had never heard him say he wanted to own anything. Yet now in his answer I heard his longing for ownership. As if he had found a new direction. He answered, "Yes, it looks good. Good."

And I said to him, "Will we keep the sheep, do you think?"

"The sheep? Oh, yes."

I did not ask him who their herder would be. I knew then, in the way you know things you have learned or been told, that it would be I. Who else? Not Papa who would probably be working at the bank in Chokecherry. Not Mama busy with homemaking and Madge and

Georgie. Not Nell who would soon be gone. And not Hobson, O sweetest God.

Sheep raising is not any play business. The herder's is not the pure, placid life some of the sentimental story writers of the golden West and purple sage country would have you believe. Sheep are like small children—dependent, independent, naughty, silly. By nature they are shy but at times ewes will fight ewes and bucks will fight bucks and these blood-in-the-eye brawlings have to be stopped either by the herder or by his dog.

Sheep are animals with odd, skittish traits. If one starts to run after something or maybe after nothing they will all take out after the starter. They will pound down a trail leading to nowhere until ready to drop in their tracks. They fall into ravines and have to be rescued. They will eat snow but are afraid of ice. They have enemies—diseases, coyotes, wolves, rattlers. . . .

Try sleeping in a feather bed sometime. Until you get used to it you will think you have been tossed into an ocean. You think you will suffocate. You sink and roll and sink again. You do not suffocate. After a while you realize you are being embraced and not choked and you sleep.

Beside Madge in our dusty, downy bed that night sleep did not come for a long time. My ordinary habits of night rest were taken from me and so my ordinary thoughts were also.

Chapter Four

The next day Hobson's throat was worse and Georgie and Madge whined with hurting bones and headache. All three alternately ran furnace fevers and rattling chills. Mama was alarmed and sent Papa to locate a doctor. When he came and did his examinations he said it was influenza, a type new to him. There was an epidemic of it raging around down on the Nebraska line.

I asked, "Has anybody died from it?"

He said, "I need to wash my hands. Get me some hot water." He left some medicine and promised to come back the next day but did not show up again for two.

By that time all in my family except me were in their beds shivering and burning.

That doctor, whose name was Iron Ross, ordered me around as if I might be his wife or nurse. "These people need to be kept clean and warm and they need nourishing food. What are you feeding them?"

"Potato soup. Biscuits. Bean soup. Oatmeal. Goat milk."

"Why don't you clean this place up?"

"I am working at it, Doctor, as fast as my legs will carry me."

"The sheets on your mother's bed need to be changed. Get me some clean ones and I'll go do it myself."

"There are not any clean ones. I have to wash some this afternoon or tomorrow. Anyway, those on Mama's bed are not dirty. That is the natural look of unbleached muslin. It is cheaper than bleached and wears like iron. We buy it by the bolt."

"This place is like an icebox."

"Don't you think I know that? I've got the fireplace and the stove in the kitchen going full blast, hot as they will go. I was up all last night hauling wood in and ashes out. Whew. I tell you, Doctor, if a rich man was to come by here this morning and take a fancy to me and ask me to marry him I think I would take him up on that proposition so fast he would think he had been attacked by a wild bull."

"Is that your ambition in life? To marry a rich man?"

"Oh, I don't know. It was up till a coupla days ago. But now we are here and I might be thinking a little bit different."

The doctor peered at me. "How is it you are not down like the rest of them?"

"Me? I am never sick. Never have been. I have never even had a cold."

"Well, maybe your time is coming. Of course I hope not."

"It isn't. I'm different. I have never had whooping cough or measles or a sore throat or anything like that. Don't you think that is strange? I do. When I die I am going to will my body to medicine science and let them find out why. I ought to make them an interesting lesson. Say, do you suppose I could do that now and get paid for it? I mean ahead of time?"

"I doubt it. I know I would not be interested."

"Maybe one of the other doctors in town would be."

"There are not any other doctors in town."

"Oh. Oh, well. Listen, Doctor, is my mother pregnant?"

"Yes, she is. You mean you didn't know?"

"Not for sure. If you've finished for this time I expect you want your fee now."

"If you have any money I do."

"Doctor, we have a little but have to be very careful with it until things are normal with us again. Do not worry, we are not debt-beats. You will get what we owe you. Do you like lambs?"

"Lambs?"

"We are sheep people. No, that is not exactly the truth. I do not want to give you the wrong impression. My father thinks he will work in the bank in Chokecherry as soon as he is well again. My grandfather Bacon was one of its founders. I am the sheep keeper here; at least I will be in a few days. I thought come spring I could give you a lamb or two for what we owe you. We will have a new crop then. Right now I don't have an extra one. Just before we got here Nell Parrott weeded our flock and took care of the fall marketing. She gave all the money she got for that to Grandpa Bacon's lawyer. He has been in charge of things up to now."

"How old are you?" inquired the doctor remembering at the last minute to leave more medicine.

Thinking one of his interests on the side might be with the school board, I told him, "Seventeen. I've finished with my schooling."

My lie did not seem to affect him one way or another. He said he would be back as his time permitted.

A houseful of sick people is cut off from reality for then the ordinary rules do not apply. Madge and Georgie found the strength to play checker games but neither, according to their rules, was supposed to win. When one did and screamed his triumph there was a pitched battle. Madge found a pile of old magazines in the cabinet under the pier mirror in the bathroom and spent much listless time snipping out coupons for free samples of Mentholatum and Golden Glint Shampoo.

Nell would not come inside our house, saying she did not want to run the risk of catching our sickness.

From her cellar she brought us apples, some parsnips and a pumpkin. I received these on the back steps. Her time was growing short. She said she was making plans to go to Rapid City for a winter-long visit with her sister there and that if I was going to take over the responsibility of caring for the sheep I should go out with her and them at least once. I longed to. I knew I should know more about that business than Ash Puck Joe's tolerances had taught me. I told her I would make out with the sheep when the time came. My patients kept me hopping.

Mama was the sickest. There was a bad time when I stood beside her bed looking down on her thinking she might die. Thinking, O God, this awful thought: We have not known each other. I have never said *I love you, Mama*. She has never said that to me. Thinking: What are we—accidents? This whole world might be an accident, an experiment somebody thought of long ago and it is failing. We don't know how to behave or take care of ourselves. We don't know how to talk to each other even at a time like this. This pretty little lady deserves more than she has been given. From us and from those before us. This house is a slap in her face from Grandpa Bacon. He knew she would come and bring us with her expecting something better. And that we would have to he-man it when we got here. And that none of us would be equipped.

There was the waiting during the blackest hours and then it was easy to think of the emptiness of life and feel its meanness and ugliness. Every time I would pass through the sitting room on my way to the other rooms it was necessary to pass by the tintype of Grandpa Bacon dangling on the wall. That old dragon. Mama had cleaned its face before her illness overcame her.

One night when the light from the moon was right I saw what I thought was a gray wolf moving in a circle on the higher grounds around our ranchstead. I thought of Ash Puck Joe who had had the experience of losing one of his best horses, a steer and four of his sheep—two ewes and two bucks—to wolves.

I took Papa's gun, loaded it and went outside and stood for a long time in the dark and the cold, looking and listening. Wolves will come up fairly close to darkened or vacated houses but I have heard and read they are generally fearful of any enclosure. Tales of this animal have made rich some of our human history yet anyone hearing its long, low, throbbing howl on a near-winter prairie night has to be reminded of self-aloneness. And danger.

Chapter Five

There is that breed of man never so pleased with himself as when called upon to deliver things which will marshal the lives of others. One day shortly before Nell's last one with us such a person came early to our home. He was a minor official from the Chokecherry Bank and Trust Company and had brought Papa a job offer. He had heard of our being in the vicinity through Dr. Ross and the man at the newspaper publishing office. He complimented Mama for being the daughter of Grandfather Bacon, declined coffee and a conference chair and, while speaking in spirited terms of the position he was offering, invited Papa to walk outside with him. It was a cold day and they stood talking on the front porch for forty-five minutes. When Papa came back in alone he said he had accepted the job.

"See?" said Mama. "I told you you would have no trouble finding employment here."

"I'll be low man on the totem pole," said Papa.

"You have been that before," rejoined Mama. "And with far less than we have here to back us up."

By that time all my patients were up and stirring around with the exception of Hobson who sat in his nightclothes before the kindled fireplace in the sitting room reading and rereading two volumes given him as farewell gifts by Maizie Green. I said to him, "Hob, you are keeping yourself sick reading that slush. You ought to dress and go outside and clear your lungs and head with some good fresh air."

Hobson looked up from his page. His smile seemed to find something in me I didn't know about. "This is not slush, it's literature. I won't waste my time explaining the difference to you. Do you have to sweep in here now? I am sick and all this dust hurts my lungs."

"Sorry. I'll open a window. There. Doesn't that air taste good? Lift your feet. Listen, Hob, I want to talk to you."

"But I don't want to talk to you," said Hobson returning his attention to his book. "You bore me."

"You can put your feet down now. Hob, I've decided not to go to school this year."

"Well, you have never been crazy about it so that won't be any sacrifice."

"I have decided I'll stay home and tend the sheep. Somebody has got to."

Still with his eyes on his page Hobson began to shake his head emphatically. "Oh, the sheep, the sheep. That's all I hear. First from Papa and now you. I hate those filthy, greasy animals. Why can't you two understand I have got to get my education? You think I want to be like Papa when I'm his age? A bank clerk?"

"Papa wants to be more than a bank clerk, Hob."

"Huh. Then why isn't he?"

"Because he has us and Mama."

"Why?" Hobson who had inherited Mama's ruthlessness as well as her looks but none of her small, good compassions seemed to have been waiting for just such an opportunity to speak his mind. He put his book aside and raised his eyes to my face. *Unendurable,* said his expression, *that is what you are to me. That is what all of this is to me.* His personality and his handsomeness, pure Bacon, fit him like a drink of water. He said to me, "Spare me your answer to that question. I know why. He has us and he has Mama because the only way he could get away from Grandpa and Grandma Drawn was to get married. He doesn't like them and they don't like him, they only pretend to. Any fool can see that. But that's not my fault. Not any of this is my fault."

"Hob, you ought to be ashamed of yourself, talking that way."

Hobson picked up his book and hurled it across the room. "I am! Don't you understand that? I am! And I hate it because I haven't done anything to be ashamed of. I'm just telling the truth. I want to be somebody and I'm going to be somebody. I refuse to be a sheepherder. Papa asked me last night and I told him no. Even if I have to leave home I won't go out and herd those sheep. I'm going to school this year, that is what I told Papa. He said all right. There. Now I've told both of you."

There could be no more discussion with him about the sheep. I could see that by the light of my own faith. This light, from whatever trusted and convincing region it came, from whatever mysterious passage, showed me this country we were in as my country, our country. I thought about it this way: Whatever we lack, whatever our mistakes will be, this is where we ought to be at this time and with these circumstances.

And I thought this: What is it? What is happening? Why am I now wanting all the old good, sloppy ways changed around? Speak, Oracle. Ah, you are not there, are you? I am whistling past a cemetery.

That day I told Mama and Papa, in separate parleys, that if they would allow it I would not attend school that year but stay home and tend the sheep. I wanted Mama to perceive, if she had not, that I was almost grown, that I could see beyond the present surface, that I understood the distances of the future. I knew her heart needed lifting.

Mama said to me, "Well, I don't know about this, Fern. Even if your father and I say yes the school authorities might say no."

"They don't know how old I am. They don't send people out asking to look at everybody's birth certificate, do they? I told Dr. Ross I was seventeen and through with my schooling. I'll bet everybody in this county has heard that story now. The doctor said I looked a little bit like Grandpa Bacon and had some of his ways. If Grandpa was here and I asked him what I'm asking you to let me do he'd say, 'Hop to it, kid, and don't let the fools stand in your way, you are showing Bacon sense now.'"

"Yes, he would say that," agreed Mama, trying to force a fried parsnip on Georgie, pointing out its nutritional qualities to him. Georgie was not having any part of the parsnip or Mama. He had not forgiven her for throwing his skull away that day in the canyon. His screams of protest were enough to waken the dead.

Ignoring them I said to Mama, "He'll eat when he gets hungry enough. Stop that, Georgie! Don't you dare kick Mama in the stomach! She is going to have another baby."

Mama's cheeks turned faintly pink. She looked at me and I thought: Now she will tell me. She sees I have grown up, that I am able now to recognize how things are, our needs. And the sense in my proposition.

But Mama, though the look that passed between us was probably the most intimate we had ever shared, only said, "All right, Fern. Try your hand with the sheep for a while."

"Mama," I said, "we need."

She said, "Yes. We need. We always have." She returned her attention to Georgie and the parsnip.

The Lord knows we needed. A fifty-pound sack of

flour will only stretch so far no matter how small you cut the biscuits or shape the loaves and there is no give to potatoes or bacon either. We had had no fresh meat since coming to Chokecherry. Clyde, our young, trained sheepdog who had cost Grandfather Bacon forty-five dollars according to Nell, fared a little better than we in that department. He was a collie variety and Nell said that several times a day while the sheep were grazing in a peaceable manner he would sneak away from them, snare a jackrabbit and have himself a quick meal in the bush.

One night during that time when our influenza siege was at its ravaging worst I took Papa's gun, loaded it, went out to the sheep pen, waked Clyde and tried to talk him into going rabbit hunting with me, but he would not leave his charges. I was afraid to go alone.

Clyde was not ever a rabbit chaser, which is an undesirable trait in any herder dog. He loved his work and had a great affection for Nell. When she left us and I became his boss he sulked and mourned for two days and sat on his haunches ignoring me and my orders, letting the sheep scatter in every which direction, watching me chase after them with contempt and satisfaction.

On the third day two bucks put a stop to this. We were on a grassy knoll, the cold sun was out, the other sheep were grazing when these two decided to have a fight. If there was a reason for it they did not let me in on it. They were feeding side by side when, of a sudden, they looked up at each other, separated, backed off to correct distances as if they were duelers abiding by the rules, lowered their horned heads and charged. On full collision course they did this several times and I was afraid one or both would be killed. The fatter one had the advantage but the skinnier one seemed not to care. He wanted victory too.

Forgetting one of Ash Puck Joe's cautions, at great peril to myself, I ran toward them with the idea, I suppose, of trying to separate them. Clyde, who had been watching all of this without any show of feeling, saw my mistake, raised himself from the ground and came racing. He nearly knocked me down, he went past me so fast. He sent the two aggressors flying down a slope and then, to show them he meant business and was still on the job, Nell or no Nell, went after them. When they came back up, Clyde between them like a truant officer, they were bleeding where Clyde had nipped their flanks but not seriously. They resumed their side-by-side grazing and Clyde's look said, *There. That's how you do it.*

In the matter of allowing me to leave school that year and stay home to tend the sheep Papa had more to say than Mama. He said, "Fern, sheep is a man's job."

I told him, "Ash Puck Joe sent his children out with his flock and it was bigger than ours. You cannot be two places at once, Papa. We want the sheep, don't we?"

"Yes," replied Papa. Like Mama, he needed to be lifted up, we all needed lifting.

We had walked out a little way from the house to have our awkward talk, climbing as we walked. Now we stood on rolling upland ground on good loam soil. To our east there was our small unidentified creek and to our west, created not by a volcano or earthquake or any other upheaval as some believe, but by the gradual wearing away of surrounding region, the soil and rock around them carried away by wind, rainfall, springs and seeping groundwater, there stood some grand specimens of the South Dakota buttes—flat-topped spurs, bare, capped with layers of sandstone or quartzite. The uncultivated land around these was covered with grasses where gullying had not occurred.

We could not see Nell or the sheep. I said to Papa, "They are probably behind those buttes. Nell said Grandpa Bacon rented this land from Indians long before he bought it. Then they sold out to him and moved on. What about my proposition?"

"I think," said Papa, "you need your education as much as Hobson."

"I can study while I am minding the sheep. A year out of school will not hurt me. We need a time to repair, Papa."

He caught the meaning of my biblical-like phrasing at once and did not smile at it. Where did it come from, *A time to repair?* Why must kids, always before sunk in self but now done with childhood affairs, always phrase themselves as prophets?

Because that's what they think they are. But kiss this kid good-bye. Playtime is over.

Due to the stressed conditions of the times there was only one rural school in operation anywhere near us. Its enrollment was poor and this was also due to the times; many families had moved away. This school was situated about halfway between us and town and the parents of the attending students had to call upon their seat-of-pants sense to get them there and back. There was this choice: Either pay the teacher or buy transportation. The parents decided the teacher was more important.

Papa said to Hobson and Madge, "Well, I can solve half this problem. I can drop you off in the mornings on my way to work but you'll have to walk back in the afternoons."

"I thought we were going to attend the school in town," said Hobson. "The one named after Grandfather Bacon."

"That one is six miles from here," said Papa.

"Lessee," said Madge. "Three miles a day. Five days a week. That is twelve, that is fifteen miles. You mean," she cried, "I have got to walk fifteen miles from school every week? With just Hobson to protect me? He can't protect me, he won't. He never has. He can't even protect hisself. I have never been a very strong little girl, you know that. What about when it snows? What about Gypsies?"

"No decent Gypsy would have you," observed Hobson.

"What about wolves and coyotes?" screamed Madge. "They attack people especially in the wintertime. I've got a better idea. We can ride Ned back and forth to school, Hobson and me."

"No, you can't," said Papa. "Have you forgotten your oldest brother is afraid of horses? And besides, Fern might need Ned here to help her with the sheep. Or your mother might have an emergency and need him."

"Oh, my feet," moaned Madge. "My poor feet. They will never last doing all that walking."

"Teach them how to run," suggested Papa. He would not give in.

Came the day, a Monday, when, as the sun cleared the tops of our hills, I watched Papa and Madge and Hobson drive off, he to his town job and they to their country school. Mama was inside the house coping with Georgie and the years of indifference that had turned a once-nice home into a house coming near to resembling a vagrant's hangout.

The sun began to etch away the night's groundfrost, I could feel the cold of the ground through my wool stockings and thick-soled shoes. I stood beside our sheep pen wishing for a reprieve. There would be no reprieve. I knew that to be a redoubtable truth for I was prairie, my roots in the roots of pioneer, and the pioneer has always known there is no easy deliverance.

So I stood beside our sheep pen preparing in my mind the day's work. With Clyde in the lead and me bringing up the rear we would take the sheep down into our valley where the grasses, cured on the ground now, had not yet been picked over and where there was water although sheep in the fall do not need water every day and just the day before Nell had had the animals near water from sunup to dusk.

Sheep like to get their daily affairs started early and they stood, all awake, waiting for me to open the corral gate. Clyde was wandering around in their midst ignoring me. This was one of those days I told you about earlier when he sulked and mourned for Nell. He pretended not to see me. He gazed at the sky. He lifted a paw to see if there might be a splinter or thorn there he might have forgotten. He sat down behind an old fat ewe. *I have decided I am not going to work today. Even a convict gets a day off once in a while. I am only a dog. Nobody likes me.*

"Clyde! Let's go, boy! Up and at 'em!"

Clyde continued to ignore me, continued to examine his paw, finally stuck the whole thing into his mouth, sucking it, making so much noise at this that the ewe he was trying to hide behind turned her head to look at him in disgust.

"Clyde, let's go! All right, you don't want to work with me today, stay here and see if I care. I'm no tenderfoot. I know how to handle sheep. Watch this."

Clyde watched, yawning. He decided to come with us but only to watch the fun.

I swung the gate of the pen wide and the animals came surging forward. In the lead there was a buck and for a reason I cannot guess he began to run in a direction opposite to the one I had planned, the others stringing out behind him. Seeing Clyde was only going to observe I ran after the buck to turn him in the right direction. His followers bunched, confused, and had to be straightened out. I had to run around and around them trying to get them headed for the valley. What a time.

Even if I had been using Ned to help me herd I

would have had a time because sheep will stand and look at a horse as if looking at nothing and the only reason they will move for their herder is to get out of the way. They are afraid of dogs and will jump to obey them. Clyde came with us that day and the next but only to skulk around the fringes of the flock watching my mistakes. Have you ever seen a dog grin?

I had remembered the wolf slying around our ranch-stead several nights before and so had Papa's loaded rifle with me and some extra ammunition stashed in a long canvas shoulder sack along with my lunch and a couple of school textbooks. The gun was cumbersome. After suffering Clyde's attitude awhile I took the weapon from its sack, showed it to Clyde and asked him, "Cur, how would you like your rear end filled with a couple of rifle rounds?"

Clyde's hairy face did not say.

The sheep, accustomed to having Clyde predict any mischief, kept eyeing him. They would not go straight down the trail toward the valley but ambled from side to side. However sheep communicate, if they do, soon the word got round that their BIG BOSS was taking him-self a holiday and *Oh, look at* LITTLE BOSS, *like Fido in a briar patch. See her leap. See her run. Oops. Now that is the second time you have fallen down,* LITTLE BOSS. *Here we are all straggled out and you cannot round us up, there are too many of us and we have all got different ideas. So the only thing you can do is let us go as we will and you follow. There is a special kind of grass that grows down there that is so good. It is hay now of course. We will be mustered there. Meet us.*

With Clyde trailing me all the while at an aloof distance I followed my sheep down into the valley. Timid by nature and distrustful and now without leadership they detoured many times. It was all Clyde could do to keep himself from streaking in to straighten them out. He did some suffering.

We reached the brown hayfield, the youngest of the animals arriving last. They all began to feed. The sun was high and warm, the weather had turned almost springlike. Clyde disappeared. I sat down on a rock to ease my aching feet and catch my wind. Peace.

I watched a ewe eat until she looked about ready to pop. There was a waterhole nearby and I watched her go to it, stick her head down to its surface and drink. When she had finished this she stepped back, threw herself to the ground and began to roll the way a dog or horse does.

I watched her. And watched. I looked away and turned back. An alarm went off inside my head. The ewe's spindly legs were in the air and she was twisting, threshing, desperately trying to complete her roll and stand again but could not. That is a fact peculiar about sheep; once on their backs sometimes they are not able to right themselves because their body gravity is different from that of a horse or dog. Especially if they have a very full stomach or are heavy with wool or lamb they will get themselves in this predicament. If the herder does not see this and take immediate rescue steps soon, very soon, the animal will die. Its inside body gases will begin to collect and swell, pressing against the vital organs, the heart and lungs and kidneys. The body will begin to puff. There will be a dreadful struggle for breath and then it will all be over.

In a jump I left my rock. On my knees beside the ewe I thrust my hands under her and began to rock her back and forth. She was heavy, almost dead weight. I did not want to see her face and avoided looking at it.

I screamed for Clyde. "Clyde! Clyde! Come help me! Oh, by the good Lord Jesus, if you don't come help me save this animal I am done with you! For good! I will blow you to kingdom come! Rock, fool! I cannot do it all! Help me! Rock!"

I could feel the blood going through my heart. There was the sound of my own heavy breathing and the fainter one of the ewe's. I think she knew she was going. Around us, close to us, the other sheep continued to munch. When a sheep feeds it does not so much bite the grass off with its teeth as tear it, jerking it off while jerking its head. There was that sound too.

It was a game of survival. Each time the ewe would rock toward me I would have to snatch my hands away for fear they would be crushed. "Rock! Rock! Get up! You aren't dead yet! Help me!"

I smelled Clyde before I saw him. There is nothing like the smell of a wet sheepdog; he had been in the water. I smelled him and then I looked up and saw him on the other side of the ewe. He was mad. He put his rump against her bloated sides and pushed and she rolled toward me. I was afraid she would roll over me and pulled back. Instead she rolled back toward Clyde. He gave me a look and went at it again, this time not sparing any injury he himself might do to the ewe. He drew his breath, scooted forward a few inches, raised himself from the ground, whirled and threw himself at the ewe. It was a strange sight. I could hardly believe it. Clyde thrust his front paws under the ewe and at the same time snapped at her nose and jaw. She groaned and rolled toward me, sides heaving. I jumped up and out of the way and Clyde rushed her again. This time he got her to her feet. The ewe staggered up, glaze-eyed. She tottered away from us and stood still. Her swollen body began to deflate. She swung her head around to regard it. Another ewe came up to her and they nuzzled. The wind made the water in the waterhole ripple. The rescued ewe went over to it, lowered her head and began to drink.

I went back to my rock and Clyde went with me. Presently I was calm enough to swallow my own kitchen-bag lunch. Clyde got half of it.

I have read stories about people who tend sheep and have been moved to wonder why the authors of these give them such saintlike personalities. There is nothing saintly about a sheepherder. They are merely human; theirs is not the golden life.

I wonder if any of the writers of these tales ever saw the inside of a sheepherder's wagon, ever experienced a prairie blizzard with riding winds up to seventy-five miles an hour while locked in one. Ever been forced to leave its wind-blasted shelter every hour or so to go out and face the gusts and wet, stinging snow, searching for lost animals.

Crawl if you must but save the animals, that is the herder's job during a blizzard. Dig in the waist-high drifts to uncover the huddled, frightened, freezing animals. Haul them out. Force them to shelter. Run. Run. Here is another drift and more animals. Haul them out. Look up and see your wagon exploding in the wind. Watch it go flying off.

That is what happened to Hobson and me during our first winter at Chokecherry. It happened in February. Black February I labeled it.

Chapter Six

Autumn is the best time of the sheepherding year for then the days are short and, barring unpredictables, neither too hot nor too cold. The ground is fat with brown feed for the woollies and they do not have to be taken to water every day. If the herder has a dog like Clyde, one with a passion for work, the days can be pleasant and repairing. Under a tree or in the shadow of a rock the shepherd can take long stretches of personal ease, study a book, think about past life, concoct a couple of recipes for the future, watch a pair of golden eagles riding an updraft—sweet Lord, what a sight.

Where once life had been all risk and hardship and treacherous wilderness Clyde and I now moved our sheep from grasslot to grasslot and the fine dust rose from the earth to coat all of us gray.

"Yo-de-lo-lay-hee-hee!" Aw, bosh, that is not any yodel. Try her again. Let her come from the chest this time. "YO-DE-LO-DA-LAY-TEE-HEE!"

The dust, the hateful dust. Why does it have to be?

Why? Girl, where is your memory?

What memory?

About dust. What Papa said about it. Take the dust of the earth away and much of our rain and snow would go. And clouds and fogs and mists. For dust is the mother of these. Around its tiny airborne particles our water forms are born. Take our dust away and the blue in the sky would drain and the colors in our sunrises and sunsets would be wiped away because it is dust that spreads and sifts and scatters the earth's and sky's color rays. There now. Is your memory freshened?

Ya. That's a good lesson.

"Yo-de-lo-da-lay-tee-hee! Dinnertime! Clyde! Come! Bean sandwiches today. Awww, come on now, you know you like bean sandwiches. Well, it's all we've got, beggars cannot be choosers. Here, pretend like this is a piece of steak, that's what I do. You had better eat it. You may not get yourself a rabbit today, they are getting wise to you."

Strong on the highlands the sun was having itself a prewinter fling. All was silence. To the north the far-separated wastes of the Badlands stood in gloomy mist.

To the east the creek twisted its patient, glimmering way.

The sheep were behaving, going about the business of fattening themselves. I watched them and thought about spring when those ewes in our flock old enough to become mothers would produce their lambs.

Clyde hated his sandwich but ate it and I ate mine. From my lard pail of water we each had a ration, he from his pan and I from my tin cup. He drank his without looking at it, he was watching the strolling sheep. I leaned toward him to pat his head and he turned and moved close to me, putting his forepaws on my shoulders, looking into my face, gazing at me in an intense, personal and almost human way. The brilliant sympathy in his eyes seemed to fit the condition. He almost spoke to me: *Friend.*

It was noonday and the sun was lemon-colored. I read another two pages in my textbook and the words slid across my mind without leaving their meaning. I watched my flock and thought about that time which would come, which had to come, when my sheep families, the rams and ewes and their offspring, would be separated, some of them driven to market. Driven to market. Hideous thought.

I am alone. We are all alone, creatures and humans. Connected but alone.

Oh, let the loneliness be.

I must not have a lick of sense. Where was I when the brains were passed out? What am I doing out here trying to learn this crazy business? I am a girl and it is time I started acting like one. I ought to tell Papa and Mama I don't want this sheep job anymore, let them sell the sheep. I should fix myself up and go to town and find myself a job. I'm old enough. I could work in a café or a store. Find myself a rich, old, unmarried gentleman. He'd dribble his gruel and expect me to drive him around in his big car. I would have to learn how; that would be all right. Old people sleep a lot, they are like babies. Mama and Papa wouldn't care. They would be glad. I could help them out, slip them a little money every Saturday. And I would be out of Hobson's way. I am partly what is wrong with him. Always laughing at him, making fun of his mistakes. Poor Hobson, he cannot even start a stove-fire. Or swallow an aspirin without gagging. And so dramatic about everything.

That afternoon about an hour before quitting time Hobson and Madge came astride Ned, Hobson riding front position trying to hide his fear of Ned with a lack of expression. He looked strained, like a cat who has just swallowed a mouthful of yellowjackets and knows inner violence is on its way. There was a slight breeze and coming up the slope Ned's beautiful red mane rippled each time he tossed his head. He was irritated because his two passengers were inexpert. Hobson kept digging his heels into Ned's flanks and at the same time kept pulling back on the reins.

When the trio was within hearing distance I called out, "Hob, give him his head! Quit pulling back on the reins, you're hurting his mouth. He sees me, he knows this is where you want to go."

They reached me and I looked up at them and said, "Get off, both of you."

Hobson said, "I will when I get ready. This beast doesn't belong to you." But he and Madge slid down and I went to Ned.

"Hello, boy. Hello, you beautiful. Aw, look. Look at this raw place on his mouth. Hobson, you dunderhead, don't you know *anything* about riding a horse? You don't nudge one to make him go and at the same time pull back on his reins so hard the bit cuts into his mouth. Pour some water from that pail there into that pan and bring it to me."

"Don't you give ME orders," said Hobson in an extraloud, ugly and vibrating tone. He went over and sat down beneath my tree letting his back rest against its trunk. He had on his after-school clothes—pants and shirt, a year outgrown, and an old red mackinaw. As if he had found in me a new source for some new inner torment he sat staring at me.

I had to go after the water for Ned but Clyde's water pan was not a suitable drinking utensil for him. Madge led him out to a nearby waterhole, let him drink, and brought him back. She, also in her after-school clothes, seemed about to choke as if she could not find air to breathe. While Ned stood switching his tail she walked around him giving him little jumpy pats. She said to me, "There's a girl at school told me a funny story about horses. There was a man lived here before the Indians moved away and he used to put the shoes on all his horses backward to make anybody who was a horse thief think they were going one place when they were going another. Isn't that funny? Haw. Haw."

Hobson set a cold stare on her and then delivered one to me. He turned his head to view the grazing sheep. "Is that all they do all day long?"

I answered, "That is their main business."

Madge, tall for her age, was practicing mounting and dismounting Ned. Squaw fashion, she boarded him from the right. She stroked his mane and walked round and round him pulling his head down to hers as if to whisper some secret in his ear and the stunning thought that she loved him came to me.

She turned and made an announcement. "I'm going to ride him back and forth to school now. Mama has already said I could because Hobson has quit and I'll be safer on a horse than on foot. The school's got a shed for horses. Of course I won't go when there's a lot of snow or when it's too cold. Then I'll stay home."

"Madge," said Hobson, his face swelled with irritation. "Take Ned and go home. I'll come with Fern." Watching our sister ride off he rose and gave the hem of his mackinaw several jerks.

Aided by the chill wind driving down from out of the northwest the warmth of the day was going. It swept over us carrying with it the last dry odors of the prairie—sagebrush, ragweed, sunflower.

My brother and I stood facing each other, maybe for a purpose, maybe for nothing. He said to me, "Mama is going to have another baby."

"Yes."

The wind, buffeting over the hillsides covered with that stubborn signature plant, the gray-green sagebrush, made them appear as great, quivering water waves. I label this many-branched shrub with its silvery foliage "signature" because where it grows the land is good for farming and stock raising.

Hobson said to me, "This morning after Papa let us out at school I went in and sat down before the bell rang and looked at my shoes."

"Hob, it isn't always going to be the way it is now. Things are going to get better. Look at the sheep down there. That's pure money."

"I hope so. I'm so tired of being poor. Anyway, I've quit school. I told Mama I wasn't going anymore."

"What did she say?"

"Not much. She doesn't want me to quit but she didn't say much. I can't learn anything there, it's for little kids. The teacher doesn't know as much as I do. We argued every day."

"About what?"

"Everything. When I was right and could prove it by the books he'd get mad and then we'd have an argument. He's not a real teacher. He got his high school diploma from the school in town and never went to college. Never even went to a normal school. Why do you suppose they're letting him teach?"

"I don't know, Hob. Maybe they couldn't find anybody else to take the job."

Hobson's expression was one of deep disgust. "That shouldn't be allowed. Teachers should know more than their students. Oh, well, that doesn't make any difference now, not to me. I've quit. What are those sheep under that little shed doing?"

"They're licking salt, it's part of their diet."

"After I told the teacher I quit," said Hobson, "I went to town."

"You walked?"

"And I looked for a job. There aren't any. I saw Papa."

"Did you tell him you had quit school?"

Hobson looked as if he had been run through by some terrible current. "No. I didn't get to see him. He was in one of those glass rooms banks have and he was getting a bawling out. I couldn't hear what for. He didn't see me. He was standing up and the guy yelling at him was sitting behind his desk drinking coffee. They wouldn't let me wait to see Papa, they asked me to leave. What do you think about that?"

My heart had begun to swing back and forth like some big, out-of-balance pendulum. For the first time in our lives my brother Hobson and I were having a meaningful conversation. Manipulated by some secret arrangement with things, this had come and I thought: I should say something strong. But what?

Hobson had turned and was looking down to where the sheep were grazing. Clyde was weaving in and out of their groupings, nudging them, persuading them to move to the thicker, unshorn weedlots.

"Clyde is smarter than most people," I said. "Sheep pick up worms if they eat too close to the ground. That is one of the reasons we keep moving them around. Ash Puck's flock got worms once and he had a sweet time getting rid of them. I wouldn't know how to treat them. I wonder if there is a county agent or somebody like that in town."

"No, there isn't," replied Hobson. "I asked. There's no veterinarian either." He had turned back to me to stare me full in the face. "The reason I asked is because I'm going to work with you now."

With a little jerk my heart stopped its crazy swinging. I wondered why I was so tired all of a sudden; the day had not been as tiring as most. Why was I so tired?

"If that's all right with you," said Hobson stiffly.

I said, "Yes. Yes, of course that is all right with me." I wanted to lie down on the ground and sleep. It was time to start home. Ahead of me Hobson loped down the hill to the shed for a look at the sheep's salt supply.

I gave Clyde my rounding-up whistle and the animals began to move, slowly at first and then at a faster pace, traveling with the colding wind. There were two glum-looking clouds hanging over our valley but before we reached our corral and Hobson ran ahead to swing its gate open the sun broke through them and there was the shine of the blue sky for a few minutes.

That night in a rare, high mood Papa sent away to a seed company for free catalogues and drew a map of our land, that part lying closest to the house, laying it out in plots: these two big ones for grain, this long one for orchard, this smaller one for house edibles. To preserve our heat we were all gathered in the kitchen. Mama was pressing the suit Papa wore to the bank every day. She glanced at his artwork several times before saying, "But North, there are only so many hours in the day. How on earth do you think you can possibly work this place up into being a farm and at the same time hold onto your job at the bank?"

"Oh," said Papa, "I can get by on less sleep than most people and the kids will help." From the flu he was pounds lighter as were Madge, Georgie and Mama.

We were not starving although a person trained in the science of nutrition might have frowned on our monotonous, starchy fare. To slaughter one of our sheep for fresh meat was unthinkable. They were our future. If we ate one we would eat two and if we ate two we would eat three. That was Papa's reasoning and Mama's.

During this time we were always perilously close to being without cash. One evening Dr. Ross came with his young wife. He said not a word about what we owed him. While he and Papa had a talk about world affairs Mrs. Doctor peered at Mama and our sitting room furnishings. She said her father, now taking his rest in Chokecherry's Garden of Memories Cemetery, had several times been partners in fruitful business ventures with Grandfather Bacon. She said, "This used to be such a lovely place. If it was mine I would think of trying to restore it."

"We are restoring it," said Mama.

Mrs. Doctor, scented and prettily outfitted in a pink silk dress and a white coat with fur collar, gave Georgie and Madge a nickel each. Before our guests took their leave Mama paid Dr. Ross what we owed him. As she handed him the money the doctor said, "Oh, now, Mrs. Drawn, you people are just getting started here so why don't you pay me half now and half later? Make it easy on yourselves."

"Thank you," said Mama. "That is a kind offer but an unnecessary one." Her pride was simple and magnificent. She had always had that but now, to go with this, there was a softening in her manner. At times she showed us an almost girlish gaiety. One day she and Georgie walked over to the creek running through the eastern portion of our sector and brought home three fish. We ate them fried for our supper that night and Mama laughed when we asked what they had used for bait and tackle. She wasn't going to tell but Georgie could not contain the secret.

He screamed with glee. "Mama made hooks out of safety pins and we found some wiggle bugs and Mama had a long stick and she made me a little one. Ohhhhh, you should have seen Mama! She JUMPED in the water and got ALL WET."

We had fish from the creek several times before our winter set in and twice had jackrabbit. Papa was not a successful hunter.

Chapter Seven

One Saturday night Papa took us all to town. It was a modest treat. We each had a vanilla ice cream cone.

Chokecherry was a place you could feel tragic about for once it had been an oasis of high revelry, host to a westward-racing civilization, a new kind of crusader streaking across the quietude of the prairies headed for the Black Hills. Gold had been discovered in those dark, silent mountains and this great, greedy human tide went after it traveling by any means they could arrange for themselves—by stage, by wagon, on mule or horseback, on foot. Outa my way, Indian!

There were ox whackers, gamblers, medicine quacks, con artists, waddies, husband hunters, historians, thieves, murderers, musicians, undertakers, hayseeds, men of the clergy, rivermen. These bulb-eyed seekers of fortune came from the south, from the west, from the north, from everywhere.

Some in this wild horde found it necessary to pass through Chokecherry and it became, for a while, a supply and refresher station. What a benefaction to the town. The cost of everything except the privilege of attending church immediately doubled, take it or leave it, bub. The incensed travelers did not haggle. They paid and rode on out.

There were always a few who tarried longer than planned, whooping it up in the saloons with their cronies and the dancing girls. The sheriff deputized two of his toughest citizens to stop the brawlings and shootings. A guard was hired to sleep inside the bank.

Chokecherry had its heyday then. It never enjoyed another. Now the street lights were dim and the middle-aged cowboys standing around on the corners with their thumbs hooked in their belts looked homeless. They blew cigarette smoke and teetered back and forth on their skinny, bowed legs. Mama said probably none of them had ever been told about the proverbial rainy day.

From way out on the moonlighted prairie there came the whistle of a night train. It would stop briefly in Chokecherry. We did not wait to see this event, we went home.

After weeks of dry days we had a heavy, scudding snow on Thanksgiving. It caught Hobson and me far out on the range and though the afternoon was still fairly young we decided to call it quits and go in.

Hobson ran down to where the sheep pawed through the falling cold stuff to get to their food. He tried to enlist Clyde's help in getting our flock started home but Clyde was blind to his motions and deaf to his voice commands and whistles. He sat with his face turned to the sky and licked the snow that fell on it.

"Jackass!" roared Hobson. "I'm as much your boss as she is and if you want to keep breathing you better understand that! It's snowing and it's going to get worse. Maybe it's going to blizzard. In half an hour we won't be able to see our noses. Get going now! Get these gumps turned around and let's go!"

Hanging onto his quiet dislike of Hobson, Clyde had his tongue out catching some of the falling flakes with it. He might have been viewing a rock or a mud butte the way he looked at Hobson. He let his expression speak for him: *I am a jackass?* Those *are gumps? Friend, you have got things slightly turned around, haven't you?* He became suddenly and passionately interested in a ewe who was having trouble wrenching food from the ground. He ambled over to her, shoved her out of his way, the dirt and snow flew backward, a clump came free and Clyde pushed it toward the ewe. Stupefied, she looked at it. It had a long root-tail on it. With no front teeth in her upper jaw—nature had replaced these with a horny pad—with only the sharp edges of her lower front teeth, to cut this big blob into pieces small enough to swallow looked like quite a lot of work and maybe a slight gamble. She decided she didn't want this lumpy, dirty handout and moved backward humping into another ewe.

The snow was fast turning into an immaculate sheet and the wind was beginning to mourn. I ran down the slope. "Hobson, quit yelling at him, he hasn't learned to mind you yet. Clyde! Let's cut out the fool now! Start picking 'em up and laying 'em down. Attaboy. That's a good boy. YO-DE-LO-DA-LAY-HEE-HEE. Round 'em up, fella. That's the stuff. That's my little man. Home! Let's go home!"

Hobson was displeasured. In the presence of a bunch of low-life muttonheads and a conceited dog I had reduced him to a rank lower than my own and it had better not happen again. He was mad and wet and cold and I was mad and wet and cold.

The snow was mantling the dry prairie range, settling on the tops of the buttes and sticking to the limbs of the trees and bushes. We were west of our creek and from where we stood could not see it. I did not think this storm was going to be any blizzard. The wind was rambunctious but not violent.

Hobson chose this time to demand my answer as to why we were not making use of the perfectly good sheep wagon sitting useless in our barn. "We ought to pull it out here and set it down and stay put for a few days at a time instead of running back and forth with these stumblebums every morning and every night. You're so smart, why haven't you thought of that?"

I said, "Later. For pity's sake, Hob, look at the weather."

"Hooey on the weather! If we had the wagon out here we'd have protection. I want to know *now* why we can't."

"You kill me, you honestly do, but all right, here's your answer. Listen quick before we both freeze to death. Our wagon has to be pulled by a horse and, if you have noticed, every night is colder now than the one before, and a horse has to be tied else he will wander away looking for a warm place to sleep, and to tie him up would be cruel. Horses feel the cold too just like humans. That is in the first place. In the second, have you looked at the inside of our wagon? It is not a hotel. It is very unprivate. I suppose we could stretch a sheet up—"

"All right," said Hobson.

"—between your part and mine and make two rooms out of it instead of one but—"

"ALL RIGHT," said Hobson. "Forget the wagon. FORGET IT. Let's go. Let's get moving while we still can. Which way? I've lost my bearings."

I said, "I have not. We go down this hill and then that way. We will go in a minute but first there is just one more thing. Don't call Clyde a jackass again, Hob. He is not one. He is a dog and a valuable one. Without him we could not do what we are doing."

I thought Hobson took my dressing-down better than most persons would have. I was a little ashamed of it. Person-to-person we were still on scrappy, gawky terms and yet something of what had been lacking between us had begun a nice, stealthy, healthy growth.

The storm turned out to be a freak. During the last twisting mile of our homeward trek the snow stopped and the wind turned, driving the lead-colored clouds back to the northwest. As Clyde led our sheep into their corral there was clear sky and again in the eastern distance our little creek was visible. Our windmill was spinning.

Hobson and I had missed visitors, Nell Parrott back from Rapid City only long enough to turn her furnished house over to its new owner, a retired professional soldier by the name of Colonel Webb Harbuck. According to Madge's description of the Colonel he was unmarried, unafflicted with any visible physical defects and so loaded down with gold nuggets he bulged. He would not take possession of Nell's place until spring. Then, if the spirit struck him, he might raise a few cattle and if the town of Chokecherry could benefit from any of his experiences he would donate them.

"He showed me a whole handful of his gold nuggets," said Madge.

I said, "Why didn't you grab one? I need some overshoes and so does Hobson. Dear God, what a day. Is it still Thanksgiving?"

"He's only fifty-five," said Madge. "I asked him. And I told him about you."

"That was mighty decent of you, mighty decent. Help me get this shoe off, I think it is frozen to my foot. No, don't twist. Pull. I wonder if the Colonel knows anything about castrating and docking lambs."

Madge had the wet shoe in her hand and sat looking at it. Her innocence was blameless. "He might. I'm sure he would. He told Mama he was a graduate of West Point."

"What is that?"

"I don't know. I think it's some kind of big school somewhere."

"Oh, that's good. Then he would know about those things. Thank God. That sure relieves my mind. I'll get him to help me come next spring. I don't think Hobson is going to last that long. I've got two feet, Madge, just like you. Do you mind?"

Madge pulled the other shoe from my foot while telling me the Colonel did not look his age except the hair in his nose was white. And he certainly was not stingy. Come. Look at all this stuff he has given us.

Through Colonel Harbuck's generosity we were now richer by Nell's washing machine minus its lost wringer, a treadle sewing machine, a dray which would come in handy for farm haulage and an old upright piano with matching stool. The piano, black and lusterless and gravely attentive, had been placed in the sitting room beneath the photograph of Grandfather Bacon.

Though Colonel Harbuck had a few years on Papa he was considerably stronger. With only a little assistance from Papa he had moved our new, heavy possessions from Nell's house to ours on the dray with a hornet's speed and when this was finished had rested but a minute. He and Nell had come in his swell car and in it they departed.

Before we ate our Thanksgiving dinner Papa demonstrated one of his talents. He sat down on the stool in front of the piano, slid back the lid which protected its keys, placed his feet on the pedals, thought for a moment, placed his hands on the keys and began to play. The instrument did not jump to musical life. It had sat too long in a cold, damp house; it had to be coaxed to perform.

"It has a good tone," said Papa, finishing his first piece and beginning another. He looked down at Georgie standing close and smiled. Georgie did not return his smile or move. He watched Papa's feet on the pedals and Papa's fingers on the yellowed keys. A strange excitement crept into his still expression. In a minute he moved to press himself against Papa's side, hiding his face in the folds of Papa's sweater.

Mama, with Hobson behind her, had come to the doorway. Mama spoke her astonishment. "Why, North, I didn't know you could play!"

"Oh," explained Papa without stopping his playing, "one time I thought I wanted to be a musician and took a few lessons. That was after I left home and I was out bumming around on my own. The lessons usually cost me fifty cents apiece; at that time I thought they were worth it and always roomed where they had a piano so I could practice."

"You never told me," said Mama helplessly as if something stable in her had been destroyed.

Georgie was pressed as close to Papa as he could get. He swung his head around and said to Mama, "Don't talk. I want to listen. Shhhhhh."

The piano fascinated him. Whenever Papa would take the time in the evenings to sit down and play it Georgie would drag a chair up close and sit there staring. If anyone spoke or made a noise during the recitals he would say, "Be quiet. Don't talk. Listen." I wondered if the next little Drawn, the coming one, would be as odd.

Mama's full-skirted dresses and aprons still disguised her condition though not as aptly as they had with Georgie. She still did not speak of it to Madge or Hobson or me and neither did Papa. It had become almost a rule for Hobson, Madge and me not to speak of it to each other. What was there to say?

Mama is going to have another baby.

We don't want another baby, we don't need one.

I know that. We all know it.

Maybe it won't get born. Maybe something will happen to it before its time comes.

You shouldn't talk that way. It's sinful.

I can't help that, it's the way I think.

Be quiet. Keep what you think to yourself.

Now each day brought a later sunrise and an earlier sundown. We rose in gray-black light, all but Georgie, and hurried to dress ourselves in the cold clothes laid out the night before. We took our turns in the bathroom, the water was icy. Papa, the earliest riser, always had a fire going in the kitchen range and breakfast started. We ate fried mush with syrup, or oatmeal and oven toast.

I gave Hobson some lessons in handling the work-horses when we would hitch one of them to the dray and go out on the range for a load of firewood. He could not overcome his fear of the heavy-footed animals. They sensed this and would paw the ground and snort and show him their teeth every time he went within two feet of them.

I was afraid to leave him alone with a tree and an axe. What if the tree should fall the wrong way and crush him or what if the axe should slip? Its sharp blade did not know the difference between wood and shoe-leather. I could not keep these worries quiet. "Hob, let me have the axe."

"No."

"You are not holding it right."

"I'm holding it my way. You want this tree down or don't you?"

"I don't. I'd like to keep it growing but we need it for fuel. Give me the axe, Hob."

"No. Beat it. Go find the sheep."

"They are not lost, I can see them from here. Give me the axe."

"No. I told you no. This is a man's job. You're not a man. When are you going to stop acting like one?" His refusal that day and from there on to let me do my share of felling trees was his submission to the new flow of feeling growing between us. It was painful to me and painful for him, I knew. It was that way because it had come late; the wasted years between us could not be re-lived. So now Hobson felled the trees, whacking their trunks into proper stove and fireplace lengths; and I stacked them on the dray, roping them to its bed; and then one of us, usually myself, would take the load home.

The land waited for the death of autumn and the birth of wintertide. We could feel it coming. One morn-ing there was a thin crusting of ice on the milk which was kept in the cellar; our faithful little doe was still providing us with it. Yet there were temperate days when the sun shone and the wind was tame and reason-ably warm. When this happened, if Hobson and I were not too far from the house with our flock, Mama and Georgie would walk out in the afternoons. Georgie was as taken with the sheep as he was with Papa's piano playing. He would break away from Mama, dart up to one of the animals, squat and try to rub noses with it. As much as the land and our house the sheep were Mama's pride.

Papa never got home from his job until nearly dark in the evenings. He would change into old clothes, eat his supper in a hurry and go at once to one of his house-mending jobs. There were rotting floorboards, ceilings which leaked, broken storm windows and doors, stained walls. Papa would stop work on these repairs for one thing—to sit down and play the piano for Georgie.

Georgie would fall asleep during the recitals, then

Papa would go outside to the sheep corral and stand for a few minutes looking at the slumbering animals. The goats slept in the barn and so, usually, did Clyde, but the slightest sound would bring him to the barn's main door which opened to give access to the corral. Clyde tolerated Papa's visits.

Mama waited, I thought, for the higher-classed people of Chokecherry to come pay visits, but they did not.

A box of curtain, upholstery and clothing fabrics arrived from Mama's aunt in Kansas City. Mama was a clever needlewoman, was even handy at hat making and shirt making, and one Sunday, all decked out in new finery, Papa, Mama, Madge and Georgie went to Chokecherry to attend church. Mama wore a blue velvet dress with full matching cape and a little blue hat trimmed in white lace. I got a report of this expedition from Madge:

"It was so-so."

"Did any of the men talk to Papa afterward?"

"No."

"Did any of the women talk to Mama?"

"A couple."

"Who were they?"

"I didn't hear them say. Oh. One old icicle said her name was Mrs. Kincaid. Her husband is Papa's boss at the bank."

"Mr. Kincaid was there and he didn't talk to Papa?"

"No."

"I wonder why. He's Papa's boss."

Madge scowled. "I think Mr. Kincaid hates Papa. Hobson thinks so too."

"Oh, Madge."

"And Mama thinks it too," said Madge. "She told Hobson. See, one time Grandpa Bacon was Mr. Kincaid's boss. And they had a fight about some money and Grandpa almost put Mr. Kincaid in jail. That's what Hobson said."

"I see. Madge, was Mrs. Kincaid nice to Mama?"

"Not very."

"What did she and Mama talk about?"

Madge cracked her knuckles. "Clothes. When the preacher went out that old icicle got down on her knees and looked at the hem of Mama's dress."

"What for?"

"How should I know? I didn't listen to all her twaddle. She wants Mama to sew for her."

"Did Mama say she would?"

Madge locked her hands behind her back and stood at the foot of the bed we shared with her face pushed forward. The country night had come. Beyond the clean, newly curtained windows the darkened fields and old hills were accepting winter. It was the twenty-first of December.

"Madge?"

"I've got a headache," said Madge. "You talk too much, you gave it to me."

"I asked you a question. Did Mama tell Mrs. Kincaid she would sew for her?"

"Yes," answered Madge. And then, as if I had made a noise at her or pinched her, she roared, "Yes! Yes! And on the way home Mama cried. Now shut up. I don't want to talk anymore. I want to get in bed and go to sleep."

Chapter Eight

During the night of the twenty-third of December the still air that had hung over our valley all the day before began to move. At first it was a slow gallop with in-between rushing sounds but soon it began to cry and bellow like some wilderness-tormented being, its long whacking gusts coming in quick succession, drowning out all sounds except their own.

Beneath our blankets Madge and I heard Papa go from his room to the kitchen. The light he carried flickered orange as he passed our door. We heard Mama call out, "North, what is it?"

Came his answer, "Just the wind and it's snowing a

little. Nothing to worry about." He was not gone long, he did not go outside.

We heard the bare boughs of the trees in the yard creak. The wind in the chimneys wailed and snarled. Madge, who believed in kid-stealing Gypsies but not in Santa Claus, began to talk about both. "Fern, you awake?"

"Half and half. But I don't want to talk."

"I'll bet there are some Gypsies out there stealing some of our sheep or one of our horses. Why don't you get up and find out?"

"Why don't you?"

"It's too cold. I'd freeze."

"I wouldn't. I'm hot-blooded. Be quiet, I want to go to sleep."

"I wonder what Santa Claus is going to bring me."

"A swift kick in the pants if you don't shut up and go to sleep."

"You and Hobson going to get our Christmas tree tomorrow?"

"Yes. I told you yes ten times already."

"This bed smells like feathers."

"Your smeller must be better than mine, I hadn't noticed."

"Boy, I'm glad it's Christmas. I don't have to go back to school now for another whole week. Mama and I are going to make vinegar taffy tomorrow. And divinity fudge to put under the Christmas tree. We're going to wrap up the pieces in red and green paper. You want to know where we got the sugar?"

"No. I wish the wind would stop. I wish you'd shut up."

"From Colonel Harbuck."

"Is he back already?"

"No, but he told Mama when he was here anything on his place we needed we could borrow so Ned and me went down to his place this afternoon and I got twenty pounds of sugar. Nell must have left it when she sold the Colonel her house. He's sure got a lot of guns."

"You went into his house?"

"Sure. He left his key with Mama."

"Good night, Madge."

"Good night. Santa Claus is going to bring you some beads that belonged to Mama when she was a girl. Before that they belonged to her aunt."

"Nothing is sacred to you, is it?"

"I'm going to get a locket and Hob is going to get a telescope. I think Mama's aunt in Kansas City must be rich, she sent us fifty dollars for Christmas. I think I'll write to her sometime. I don't know what Georgie and Papa are going to get; I couldn't find their presents. Good night."

"GOOD NIGHT, MADGE."

It was true our bed smelled. I wondered how old its feather mattress was. I inched over closer to Madge and presently her warmth and punctual snorings helped me to sleep.

The next morning when Hobson and I went out to the sheep corral the first thing we saw was a trail of claw marks and triangular heel prints running round and round the enclosure, imprinted in the lightly crusted snow; then a burrowing belly hole between ground and the protecting wooden panels and fence; and then, inside the corral, two ewes lying still and stiff. The red, stained snow around them told its own monstrous story. The head and breast of each of the dead ones had been crushed and then opened. The preyer had eaten well.

Viewing this foul sight Hobson stood like a person shot but unable to fall.

I felt the color in my face go and I thought: Why don't I just go on and keel over, that is what a normal girl would do. A thing like that just takes your breath away.

It is a severe and good truth that people learn to stand together in the face of dangers. They forget the defects they have resented in their fellows. Hobson now showed me a new level of himself.

We were out earlier than usual that morning since our plan for the day was to take our flock to newer, outpost pasture near water. It was not yet real, full daylight, the whitened ground created a false dawn. There was still some wind but this had gentled. The snow had stopped. In the east, beyond our creek where the sun would appear when it was ready, some stars lingered.

The sheep were coming from their shed into the corral. Without any show of feeling they moved past the two dead ewes toward Hobson. They wanted their freedom and food.

Hobson disregarded them and went to the hole in the fence. He stood looking down at it and then removed his wool gloves, squatted, gazing at the wooden panels that had been punched askew, plucking at the broken wire mesh fencing with his fingers.

I said, "What is it?" and he came back to me to show me wisps of snagged fur.

"Our killer is a gray wolf," he said. And in the next breath asked, "Where is Clyde?" and beat me to the barn door which the wind had closed.

Clyde was lying inside the door with his head resting between his paws. We thought he was dead. I knelt beside him and put my hand on his bloodied head. He did not whimper or open his eyes. I could not feel any breath in him. He was badly mangled. I said, "Oh, Hobbie, he is dead."

Hobson ignored me. He had crouched down on the other side of Clyde and was doing some careful examining.

In a minute I said, "You can stop. He is not breathing. He tried to save the sheep. For us. And he got himself killed trying. Why didn't one of us hear and come out? I heard all the racket, so did Papa. He even got up and looked out. What if he *had* come out? The wolf would have killed him too!"

"Wolves won't attack humans," said Hobson. He had assumed the cool, professional posture of an examining physician. If he had had a stethoscope around his neck he might have been Grandpa Drawn.

I said, "They will too! They'll kill anything. If you'd read some real history once in a while instead of that junk you've always got your nose stuck in you'd know that. There are some famous wolves in the history of this state and what made them famous is their killing. Don't you know about the one who did so much killing the government sent a man out here to track him down and kill him, and there was another one—"

"Shut up," said Hobson. Not ready to admit Clyde was gone he was bent over him searching for life signs. His hand found one. "Wait," he said. "I feel his pulse. Here. Here it is. His heart is still beating."

"No. He is dead. Look at all the blood. How can he be alive? Oh. Oh. It's Christmas and my dog is dead. Oh, Clyde, I loved you so and I never told you. You didn't know it and now it's too late. Oh. Oh."

Hobson ignored this outburst. He was calm as Mama would have been calm. In a normal tone he said, "Stop that. You want to bawl and carry on do it later. I told you Clyde is NOT dead but he is going to be if we don't do something and do it quick. Run to the house and get Papa. Tell him to get out here fast. Bring an old blanket or a quilt. Tell Mama we're going to need some hot water and some clean rags. Medicine too, any kind. Get going. GET GOING!"

Afterward Madge said I started screaming my bad news before I hit the back steps.

We made a hammock-litter from a quilt snatched from one of the beds and after Papa and Mama had determined moving would not do him further injury carried Clyde into the house and made a recovering place for him in a corner of the warm kitchen. With some green soap from our medicine cabinet, warm water and a solution of hydrogen peroxide Papa cleaned his wounds. The peroxide boiled up white in the raw, broad gashes and Clyde opened his eyes, sorting out our faces until he found mine. He tried to stick his tongue out to lick Papa's hand but his blood loss had weakened him too much; he couldn't accomplish this. With an eyedropper Mama dribbled warm water with some paregoric mixed in it into his mouth and presently he laid his head to one side and went to sleep. Mama covered him to the neck with a cotton blanket.

The bad part then was I had to leave Clyde and get on with my day's work. Papa said when he got to town he would try to locate Dr. Ross and ask him to come out for a look at Clyde. I said, "He is not a veterinarian, he will not come."

"He might surprise you," rejoined Papa. Before he left to go to his own job he helped Hobson and me dispose of the slain ewes. We wrapped the mutilated bodies in burlap, hitched one of the workhorses to the dray and took our grisly burden to a dense thicket between our house and Colonel Harbuck's intending to dig a grave and bury the ewes but we could not. The ground was frozen and Hobson broke his shovel. We had to leave the dead sheep there on the open ground. Papa covered them with tumbleweeds.

On the way back to the house I said to Papa, "That killer will be back."

"I don't think so," said Papa. "It took a lot of nerve for him to do what he did last night. Usually wolves will not come up so close to a house unless it's empty, and they are afraid of being trapped in any kind of pound."

"I think this one is a killer. I think he might be an outlaw like that one they called Three-Toes. I read where Three-Toes killed thirty-five sheep in one night just for the heck of it. Thirty-five. That's what I think our wolf is like. I think he likes to kill just for the heck of it. Why did he have to kill two of our sheep? One would have been enough for him, I don't care how big his stomach is. He almost killed Clyde too. He might still die. I don't see how you can be so calm about this."

"I am not calm," said Papa in a voice hard with authority. "I am as mad over this as you are but I cannot change animal nature. No one can. And I can't quit my job and go out on any wolf hunt either."

"Give me your permission and I'll go out after him," I said.

"You don't have it," said Papa. "I told you you could take my rifle with you when you go out with the sheep but only for self-protection."

Before setting out with our flock that morning Hobson and I filled in the belly hole and patched the corral fence. Mama took over Papa's morning chore of milking our doe goat and supplying her and her buck with fresh warm water. Goat raising is a story all by itself. Somebody had had the sense to remove the horns from both of ours, probably at birth.

We got a late and muddled start. At the last minute we had to run back to the house for our sack containing our lunch sandwiches and two books. Hobson carried this and a hatchet while I took our lard pail of drinking water and the rifle. Animal nature or no animal nature, permission or no permission, I meant to keep a sharp lookout for our killer-wolf and, if I could, destroy him.

Herding without a dog has to be one of the meanest tasks the Lord ever thought of for a human being. That day I assumed Clyde's position at the head of our procession and Hobson brought up the rear.

At first our charges were wary. Sensing something was different they had to be driven from their pen—they kept looking around for Clyde to come bounding from the barn or the house. Outside their pen they milled around pawing in the snow as if they had never seen any before. Hobson and I might have been parts of the general landscape for all the attention they paid to us. I whistled and shouted starting orders and the sheep stood. I started out across the field surrounding their pen thinking they would pick up and follow. They did not. It took a tumbleweed, at least four feet in diameter, to turn the trick. Like some gray daytime ghost being pushed and made to leap by the wind it came rolling out from behind the rear of the barn and moved toward the nearest of the sheep. They jumped back from it, all but one buck. In his lifetime he must have seen hundreds of these great, crackling balls yet he had never learned to trust them. He picked up his feet and lit out. I had to jump out of his way. As he bounded past me I heard his wheezing and muttering. The other sheep followed suit, at first stringing out, then scattering, then forming a column. The buck was now in charge. He swung out first to the right and then to the left and the others followed, tongues hanging out and sides heaving.

They were running downslope, some of them slipping over the frozen snow as if skating. What a silly sight. They were headed for the creek and, seeing this, I fell back.

Hobson came steaming up to me. "They're heading for the creek."

I said, "Let 'em. If I don't miss my guess it will be iced over a little and they will not cross it unless they are forced. They are afraid of ice. Whew. Look at them run. That crazy buck."

Playing follow-the-leader the sheep pounded across the valley floor. The buck had seen the creek. He applied his brakes and then swerved off to the right. He halted, gave a couple of satisfied jumps, looked down and began to paw the snow, digging out his breakfast. This one was vain. During the months of October and November he had courted the best ewes in the flock. Come spring, with luck, we would see many little images of him.

Sure enough the creek was frozen along its banks. Hobson and I had to break the thin ice with some stout lengths of wood so the sheep could have water along with their food. Soon the scene was one of peace. The sun came but not strong enough to do any amount of thawing. Hobson and I cleared a place big enough for a small fire and sat beside it on two log pieces reading our books and watching the sheep.

Hobson was fretful. He could not keep his mind on his reading and kept interrupting mine. "I have been thinking," he said.

"Good."

"I have figured out why Grandpa Bacon left us this place."

"So have I."

"I'd sure like to show him up."

"You think I wouldn't?"

"Of course he's dead."

"Very."

"But wouldn't it be good if we could make a fool of him?"

"I'd rather do that than marry a millionaire."

Hobson leaned forward to stir our fire with a stick. Sometimes he used a little trick with his eyes to let them speak with more meaning than his words. "I've been thinking since we've got this place and those sheep down there we might as well make them pay off. Scientifically."

"Scientifically. Sure."

"I mean," said Hobson, shoving his words at me, "we ought to have some books or something to go by. Or maybe get somebody to come out here to show us what we might be doing wrong."

"Books cost money, Hob, and you will not find anybody to come out here and show us how to do anything without pay. What do you think we are doing wrong?"

Hobson held his irritation in check. "I didn't say we were doing anything wrong. I said we might be. I said since we have the sheep and this place we ought to try to be scientific. What about when spring comes?"

"What about it?"

"That's when the lambs are born, is that right?"

"Yep."

"And we'll have to shear them too, is that right?"

"Yep."

"I don't know a thing about either one of those things."

"I do. From helping Ash Puck Joe."

"How many times did you help Ash Puck with his lambing and shearing?"

"One."

Hobson stirred the fire again but did not add any more fuel to it. I did not want to admit to him how little I actually remembered about both these proceedings. The how-to of things is often realized during the twenty-third hour.

The sheep were moving downstream. We threw snow on our fire and went with them, I holding the rifle on the wary, watching the hills and clusters of dark creekside thickets for any signs of the wolf.

To walk across this pleasant, full-of-surprises land is to walk where once the proud Dakota Indians had ranged, where once great herds of buffalo, deer and antelope had been a common sight. The land is still there, enduring. Of the struggle for it between Indian and paleface there remain some occasional signs for the careful and caring observer: some arrowheads lying in a crevice, here and there some little piles of marking stones—dead echoes of things which probably will not ever be duplicated.

About two o'clock we found our Christmas tree. Hobson said he thought it was a juniper. Using his hatchet he took only its top. I said to him, "Madge wanted a big one."

And Hobson said, "I don't care what Madge wants, I am not going to chop the whole thing down. That's waste."

The sheep did not give us any trouble during the homeward drive. As we neared the house Madge came running out to meet us. "Guess what happened!"

Hobson handed her the little tree. "Santa Claus came early."

"Haw!" cried Madge. "Haw! You are funny, Hob."

I said, "Clyde died."

"No," shrieked Madge. "No! The doctor came and sewed Clyde up. It took a hundred and forty-eight stitches. He isn't going to die. Guess what happened. Georgie knows how to play the piano! He learned all by himself!"

I said, "Wonderful. That's just wonderful."

Madge brought the little tree up holding it in front of her face. She touched her nose to the tip of one of its branches. Her smile had fallen. "You don't believe me, do you?"

"Sure we do. Why shouldn't we? But right now we're tired and want to get home."

"You don't believe me. I can see you don't but you just wait till tonight. Georgie's going to play and Mama's going to make everybody sit down and listen. Then you'll see." Cradling the little tree in her arms Madge whipped around and loped away down the trail. There was the smell of more snow in the air.

That night after supper Georgie importantly climbed up onto the stool in front of the piano and played for us, one hand at a time. He had only composed one tune of single notes but it was a real one. We were obliged to listen to it six times.

Chapter Nine

The Good Man must have had His reasons for giving us winter. Probably in this harsh and aloof time when frozen birds sit in frozen trees and the nights come long and there are the brutish winds and much of life seems to be at check there are lessons to be found.

Our winter that year was a load. The weather was mild up until the second week of January but then it was snow on snow and the racing winds piled the stuff against the sides of the house in such drifts we could see nothing from the windows unless we stood on chairs.

On the lee side of the barn, its hood covered with layers of newspaper, gunnysacking and a sheet of waterproof canvas, our car stood anchored. No amount of coaxing could make its engine fire. Papa said, "Well, that is that for now anyway," and thereafter rode one of the workhorses to and from his job in Chokecherry. They were less valuable and tougher than Ned. There was a stable not far from the bank where Papa worked and for twenty-five cents a day he housed his mount there. The owner of this establishment provided drinking water but not food. Papa had to take that from our barn supply and during the time allotted him for his own lunch walk to the stable to feed the animal.

Mama asked Papa what his coworkers and employers, especially Mr. Kincaid, thought of his means of transportation and he answered, "Jenny, I haven't asked them and I don't intend to. I don't want to worry you but I think Kincaid is just itching to fire me now that I've got his accounts all straightened out."

Startled, Mama looked up from her cooking. "You mean because of that old trouble between him and my father? Oh, North, that was years and years ago. Mr. Kincaid is an old man now. I think he's forgotten all about that."

"Well," said Papa, "maybe so." By him, that day, Mrs. Kincaid had sent a box of dress patterns and fancy materials to Mama along with word she would be out for fittings as soon as the weather cleared.

Madge's school closed for about ten days. She was a willing enough mother's helper but jawed when the rest of us tracked her clean floors or rumpled our beds too much. She said to me, "Your side of the bed always looks like a rat's nest when you get through with it. Why can't you be still when you sleep?"

"Because I'm not a mummy."

"I have to take our bed apart and put it back together again every single day."

"I'm sorry you have such a tough life."

With a pleased expression containing some clever knowledge Madge said, "Colonel Harbuck is coming back pretty soon. Mama had a letter from him. He's bored in Rapid City."

"I wish I could be bored in Rapid City."

"If I tell you a secret you won't get mad at me, will you?"

"What secret?"

"No. First you have to promise."

"All right. I promise."

"I sent Colonel Harbuck a valentine."

"You what?"

"I made it myself. Papa mailed it for me. I told him it was just a letter to the Colonel. Papa knows I like to write letters."

"Valentine's Day is not until next month, Madge."

"I know it but I like to get things done."

"I think there is one country," I said, "where they brand people on the forehead for telling lies."

"I didn't tell Papa any lie," protested Madge. "Not exactly."

"A valentine is more than just a letter, Madge. You are only supposed to give them to special people."

"Well," said Madge, "Colonel Harbuck might be special to us. Sometime."

"How?"

"I signed your name to my valentine," confessed Madge. Mama was teaching her how to darn socks and she bent to her task, needle flashing, a picture of the most confounding form of innocence. What do you do with a child like that? You let it go, that is all I can advise.

Our pipes in the house froze. For water we had to lug in buckets of snow and melt them on the kitchen range top.

Hobson and I took the sheep from their pen every morning but they were not inclined to do much traveling in the deep snow. Grumbling and groaning they wandered around the house and barn pawing for buried food. We shoveled the snow from their pen and forced them to the higher, windswept grounds. We did not lose any which was a wonder. We counted them every morning and every night. None appeared to be diseased or undernourished. The Lord watches over the ignorant.

I knew this was a heart-sorrowing time for Clyde. Every morning he whined to go with Hobson and me but instead had to lie in his corner allowing his wounds to heal. To have a few private minutes with him every night after the others were asleep was an ease I did not want to have to explain so we did our visiting in whatever natural light conditions offered:

Hiya, boy. You weren't asleep, were you?

No, just lying here trying to get well. Talk about a dog's life.

Did you sleep today like I told you to?

Some. The little boy keeps me awake with his piano banging and he and the little girl fight a lot. You are pretty.

Awwwwww.

And you smell good.

I just had a bath a while ago with lemon soap. Washed my hair too. Look what I brought you.

What is it?

It's your supper.

No, it is not. It's yours. I had mine hours ago.

So did I but Mama put too much on my plate so I saved this for you. It's beef heart. Delicious. Eat.

You are so good to me.

I like to be good to you. I love you. Oh, you can stand up! Wait, let me put on a light, I want to look at you. Clyde. Clyde? What is it, boy?

I don't know. I hear something. Shhhhhh. Something is outside.

In the lukewarm kitchen I crouched beside Clyde standing weakly on his pallet with his head raised. I listened and heard nothing. I put a hand on Clyde's back and felt him trembling. The hair on his neck was bristling. And I heard it then, what Clyde was hearing, faint, terrorized cries mixed with the pulsing wind, coming either from the barn or the sheep pen. I whispered to Clyde, "Lie down. Don't bark and DON'T try to follow me."

Clyde sank to his pallet. He put his head between his paws. Papa's rifle hung in its rack above him and I stepped over him and took it down. My thought was this: The wolf is back and he is out there killing more of our sheep. Watch out, killer. Here I come and this time it is going to be YOUR carcass.

Holding the rifle I started toward the back door, moving through the gray darkness with caution. A finger on my elbow and a voice, Papa's voice, soft and low in my ear, almost made me jump from my skin. "Give me the rifle, Fern."

I whispered, "I think the wolf is back again, Papa."

"Is this thing loaded?"

"No, you told me to always unload it so I . . . Yes, it's loaded. Today I forgot. Papa, wait a minute. I'm a better shot than you."

"Oh, be quiet," said Papa, whispering too. He was barefooted and, like myself, clothed only in outing flannel pajamas. He crossed the room to the back door, opened it and stepped outside onto the porch. He tried to motion me back but I was as determined as he.

The porch and steps had been cleared of snow. All the while trying to order me to go back, go back, with sharp motions, Papa started down the steps. I would not go. I matched his footfall with my own. The lighted moon made the hard-packed snow in the yard glitter and now the cries from the sheep pen had stopped. I was not aware of the cold. I felt the blood rushing through my heart and between lulls in the wind I felt the silence and the danger. I thought I smelled the wolf.

The crusted snow supporting our weight, Papa and I moved across the yard to the barn and entered its side door. This was no feat and created no sound since either Hobson or Papa had cleared the entrance for easy access. The horses and goats were asleep in their stalls. The barn was fairly warm and not dark as you think of dark. There was enough light in it for us to see. We went across its hay-covered floor to its main door which provided unhindered entry to the corral. Papa gave it a gentle push with his palm and it swung out and we saw the wolf then, standing in the center of the sheep pen with his head lowered over a still form. Why the other sheep had not retreated to their shed beyond the corral I cannot guess. They were all awake, standing around the arena with their bodies pressed against one another and against the board fencing, and only every second or so did one of them whimper.

What a strange and evil sight this scene was. What was this pack-living hunter doing there alone? Was he mad? Rabid?

He was big. Probably he weighed around seventy-five pounds and measured seven feet in length including his bushy tail. To me his head looked enormous. His legs were robust and his feet were large. He had a deep, narrow chest. I knew he was male; the female of this truly wilderness animal is smaller.

He had lifted his head. Did he see us? Or smell us? He was bold, moving around to stand between us and his kill, protecting it. Papa and I were standing in the shadow of the barn door.

The wolf had seen us. He took a step forward. And another. Papa brought his rifle up setting its stock against his shoulder. I heard his breath and my own.

The wolf took another step and his voice came from his throat. The moon put a path of light between us. I heard the thunder of Papa's shell and saw the wolf as he leapt, whirled and fell.

"Wait," said Papa. "Wait. Let's make sure."

The wolf was not feigning. He was dead. The sheep he had killed was a young, pregnant ewe. Papa and I dragged the bodies of our criminal and his victim from the corral to the yard, covered them with the canvas and gunnysacking taken from the hood of the car and left them there for the balance of that night.

To view an untamed, dead being such as the gray wolf, to know that you have had to outwit and destroy him, is profoundly troubling. Is it because within the still gaze we see old, old secrets, veiled and impassable and menacing to us, and we think we will never touch them? That the different banners man and wild animal live under will never be explained? That we will never be able to live together in sure peace?

Hobson, Papa and I took the body of the wolf and the ewe to the thicket early the next morning on the dray. I thought Hobson was relieved he had slept through all the commotion of the night before though he said to Papa, "Why didn't you send Fern to wake me up? It was my place to be out there with you, not hers."

The bodies of the first two slain sheep were gone. Again we had to use tumbleweeds for makeshift graves.

All the time we were about this Papa talked to us about spring, about how the fields and haylands, the vegetables and fruit gardens would look when planted and beginning to grow. This dream of his sounded immense to me and near to impossible. Hobson went right along with it, nodding agreeably, adding his own comments to Papa's. He was still the aristocrat, more Bacon than Drawn, but now it was hard to think of him as the silly boy who had made himself sick over love for Maizie Green. He was toughening and wising up now, as able to envision the future as Papa. Somewhere along the line the bonds holding him apart from our father had fallen. Papa's dream, dangled before Hobson's eyes, was as real to him as the horse drawing our dray homeward through the snowfields.

"Yo-de-lo-da-lay-tee-hee!"

"Lord have mercy," murmured Papa.

"She is never going to grow up," commented Hobson, showing Papa how expert he had become at horse handling.

And Papa said, "Wouldn't that be nice?"

Came February and a chinook. This snow-eater, these warm, dry winds sweeping down from the eastern sides of the Rocky Mountains blowing from a westerly direction, brought thawing. Where the ground was bare of wintered vegetation covering, this meant mud and was a trial for Hobson and me but not for the sheep. Sure that spring had come again, they surged from their pen each morning at daybreak and took off on a rejoicing run like so many school-freed children, slipping and sliding around in the greasy mud, falling in it, kicking up gobs of it. When they reached grass they stopped, lowered their heads and went to work like machines. I reckoned the temperature teetered back and forth between ten and forty-five degrees. There is no right clothing for chinook weather. One hour you freeze and the next you roast.

During this kind time the sheep worked so hard and fast at their mowing it was necessary to move them farther and farther from home each day and I began to think maybe Hobson was right, that we should make use of the sheep wagon to cut down on all the traveling back and forth. Papa balked at the notion but in Mama we now found a surprise ally. She overrode Papa's objections and one morning we hitched one of the workhorses to our prairie wagon loaded with dishes, cooking utensils, bedding and enough food and drinking water to last four days, and Hobson, showing off a little, drove it from the yard and out onto the range. Clyde and I followed with the sheep. He had regained all his old health and zip and since this was his first day back at work he was wild with excitement.

When I let him into the sheep pen he ran like a shot to the center of it, danced around for a minute and then began barking orders. *Get up, get up, it's time to go. Don't you see the day coming? Up, up, time is wasting!*

The sheep were already up and did not need his urging. They told him so with their irritated looks. Clyde worked fast, emptying the pen, but not so fast as to cause them to bunch. Mama and Papa were standing on the back porch watching, waving to us, calling, "Be careful. Stay safe. Keep your door locked at night. Take care of each other."

At the last minute Madge came roaring out to me. "Wait! You forgot some things!" She thrust a bar of soap and two books at me.

I said, "But I put these in the wagon. Why'd you take them out?"

Glum-faced, Madge dropped her hands to her sides and stood looking at me, something in her eyes stirring. In the voice of an accuser she said, "Because I need to tell you something but there's always somebody around listening. Listen here, Fern, I think Mama is going to have her new baby pretty soon."

Clyde was urging the sheep up the slopes. They are like goats. They like to climb but at the same time are afraid of what they might meet on a hilltop unless shown by their herder or dog-boss there is nothing to fear. They were angling out, avoiding the slope though they had been over it a thousand times, and Clyde was tearing back and forth trying to do both his job and mine.

I said to Madge, "How soon? Do you know that? Did you hear her tell Papa?"

"No," said Madge. "I didn't hear her tell Papa. I heard her tell Mrs. Kincaid. She came for some of her clothes yesterday. She was mad because Mama didn't have them all finished. Mama told her she'd have them all done by next week. After the baby came."

"Madge, I want you to go back and tell Papa what you just told me. Don't let Mama hear you but tell him."

"Mrs. Kincaid told Mama it wasn't anything to have a baby. She said farm women did it all the time. By themselves."

"You tell Papa. I've got to go."

There were tears in Madge's eyes. "I tried already, but he was so busy helping you and Hobson with the wagon he didn't hear me. He wouldn't listen. Some women die when they have their babies. That happened to a girl at school. When she was born her mother died. You don't have to go with the sheep. Clyde and Hobson can take care of them."

"Madge, it isn't going to happen today. Mama's all right. See her there on the porch? You can tell Papa to-night. Be sure and do that, you hear? Hobson and I will be back in four days. I *have* to go with the sheep. They mean everything to us."

Madge's face was rigid. Her nose had turned an ugly shade of red. "Go," she said. "Go with the sheep. That's where you want to be. That's all you care about, those old sheep." Mama and Papa were still standing on the porch watching and for their benefit Madge skipped away from me backward while drying her tears and composing her face, then wheeled and hopscotched back to the house crying, "Haw! Haw! Oh, that was funny!"

The sheep had gone over the top of the first slope and were running toward another. Hobson had got a good start on us with the wagon. Every once in a while I would see it as it topped a rise in the land and then it would disappear again.

There is no telling how much Grandfather Bacon

had paid to have this little home-on-wheels built. It had some nice touches. There was a step affixed to a hinge so that, when not in use, it could be folded back under the Dutch door which was not centered directly over the wagon tongue but slightly to its right. There were two stationary benches for sitting and sleeping, a small gate-legged table that could be dropped from the wall or folded up to allow more room, two rear windows, a floor well concealing a storage compartment for supplies and food and water, a dish and cooking utensil cupboard with retaining edges and a stove equipped with a stove-pipe which stuck up through the roof of the vehicle. We remembered to take along a shovel and our axe. For privacy Hobson strung a rope line down the center of the wagon and hung a bed sheet over it.

But for all its cheeriness and attention to design our prairie home was flimsy as chaff in the wild storm that hit us two days later, a Paul Bunyan–sized blizzard with winds I estimated to be up to seventy-five miles an hour, temperatures far below the zero point and wet snow and sleet hurling past our wagon in straight lines. Like a paper boat caught in an eddy our wagon rocked back and forth and sideways.

It is the violence of the wind that gives blizzards their black name and this giant deserved the blackest. Its suffocating force drove the sheep from their winter bed-ground which was a low, hollowed-out place in the land around the wagon. They took shelter wherever they could find it: in draws, in blown-out water holes, between rocks, under banks. They buried themselves in the snowdrifts; you can imagine their desperation. Hobson and I were up all night digging them out of the drifts, driving them to safer shelters.

We lost our wagon to the wind. Clyde, Hobson and I were inside it taking ourselves a five-minute rest when there came one unusually violent blast and Hobson yelled to me, "We've gotta get out of here! Grab the shovel! The shovel! I've got the rifle! No, don't try to save anything else! Out! Out!"

The three of us made it just in time. Came another long, vicious blast and we saw our wagon blown sky-high. I saw its ribbed roof, shorn of its canvas spreading, go sailing out across the prairie followed by a wheel. What a terrifying sight.

We also lost our horse; we found him the next morning plastered against a rock. His neck was broken. We only had time to view him for a minute for Clyde was barking. He had found more sheep in the drifts and was barking for us to come with the shovel.

We only lost one of our sheep—the vain buck. I could not bear to look at him. Hobson covered him with snow and we left him.

There is no way to describe a blizzard such as that one. Words cannot reconstruct it. You have to see it for yourself.

Chapter Ten

Those with the gift for setting their gab onto paper did a duty to history when they recorded the victories and failures, the adventures and misadventures of the old, rambunctious West. The list could stretch a prairie mile and not all these exploits are to be admired.

I, for one, cannot feel pride when I read of the time gold was discovered in the Black Hills and a great, frantic crusade of fortune seekers came raring across the plains, unmindful and uncaring that the majestic and peaceful land they profaned on their destructive way to the glory mountains was not theirs but the property of our First Americans. The hostilities between red men and white were terrible and drastic. It was tomahawk and bow and arrow against trigger and you can imagine the ghastly wakes of battle.

Still, glorious and inglorious, all that is a part of our unchangeable past.

It is a pity, in my opinion, that only remote accounts of a handful of the women of that time and region received recognition. It is possible the reason for this was some were merely products of campfire gossip but I like to think there actually existed such female intrepids as Bull Train Alice, Nugget Bessie, Painted Creek Polly, Full House Florrie and Mama Hunkpapa.

Mama Hunkpapa, whose real name was Ernestine Fleenor, came to South Dakota alone from Philadelphia where she had been a poetess and teacher of the violin. It was her intention, or so goes the story, to deliver a little culture to the opening West but this aim did not pan out. Whereupon she made other arrangements for herself which did. She cut her long, coppery hair, persuaded a mule skinner to teach her how to ride a horse and use a gun, donned buckskins and went to work for a cargo hauling outfit.

As legend has it around Chokecherry Ernestine was a crack shot and was regarded by both the Indians and whites as a holy terror. Those who knew her well enough to risk it called her "Ernie" until she married an Indian known as Charlie Hunkpapa. Theirs might not have been the greatest love story ever told but they lived together happily and in peace in a sod house, which is a drab, squat structure constructed of dirt blocks so densely interwoven with tough roots of prairie grass that chunks of it are solid enough to be easily cut from the ground and laid, brick fashion. The walls of such economical places of abode have a nice natural color and do not crumble with age but strengthen. Their roofs are brush or tree limbs or cheap slab lumber covered with dirt.

Ernestine and Charlie built their house on virgin prairie above Tum-Tum Creek. What did they use for money? Nobody seems to know or care. Why Ernestine was nicknamed Mama Hunkpapa remains another mystery since she never bore Charlie any children. Maybe this was a joke. Well, that makes a good story, doesn't it?

The badge of Dakota country lies in its victory over time, lies much in the dogged courage, the spirit of work and adventure and the tough endurance which possessed and still possess its people. We do not pretend the blithe view. We have our winds, droughts, heat, grasshopper hordes, blizzards, coyotes, wolves, rattlesnakes and dust storm scourges. We know there are times when we are all in terrible danger. . . .

During the blizzard to which we lost our sheep wagon, one of our workhorses and our vain buck—that year I was fourteen and Hobson sixteen—a new member was added to our family: Ruth Patience. Hobson and I were out on the range in the blizzard when this event took place. Madge gave me her account of it:

"Well, when the storm started Mama was awful worried about you and Hobson and Papa. She went out to the barn and put Ned's saddle on him but then pretty soon came back in and said for Georgie and me to stay in the kitchen where it was warm but not go near the windows. Then she went to her room and locked the door. It got dark and Papa didn't come home and we were scared. I couldn't see through Mama's keyhole because she stuffed it with a rag and Georgie kept asking me what was wrong and I didn't know what to tell him or what to do and the wind got worser and worser and it got darker and darker so then I made Georgie and me a bed on the floor in front of the stove and I told him a ghost story. About the man with the golden arm. You know the one?"

"Ya."

"*Who stole my golden arm? Whoooooooo? Whooooooooo stole my golden arm? Whooooooooo? you did!*"

"Madge."

"What?"

"Shut up."

"Then we went to sleep. Then we heard somebody banging on the door. Guess who it was?"

"The man with the golden arm."

"Naaaaaaah. It was Papa."

"Papa came home in the storm?"

"Sure," replied Madge regarding me as calmly as she would a stick of firewood. "He knew Ruth Patience was coming and he knew he had to get here to help Mama. He got lost in the blizzard, that's what took him so long. He doesn't work at the bank anymore. Mr. Kincaid fired him."

"WHAT!"

"Don't yell. You'll wake up Mama and Ruth Patience. Are you sick?"

"Ya."

"Where?"

"I dunno. Everywhere. Our wagon blew up."

"With you in it?"

"No, we were out picking flowers."

"You want a cup of coffee?"

"Who made it?"

"Papa."

"Then I'll have some, thank you."

Madge set a cup of black coffee in front of me. "There's no sugar. Georgie ate it all."

"Well, maybe it won't kill him."

"And no milk. Our goat's gone dry. Now we'll have to buy it till her kid comes."

"I don't care."

"How do you like the name of Ruth Patience?"

"Love it."

"She's not very pretty."

"Good. Then she'll match you and me, won't she? Is Mama all right?"

"Oh, sure. I cooked her breakfast and took it to her and now she's asleep. What're you bawling about?"

"Oh, that's just something I do when I'm happy."

"The wind swiped some of your hair."

"I know it."

"Does it hurt?"

"No."

"Papa went out looking for you and Hob hours ago," said Madge. "The storm's over now. He'll be back pretty soon, won't he?"

I said, "He's back now. He and Hob are out in the barn. They'll be in, in a minute."

"Georgie!" shouted Madge. "Papa's back!"

"I don't care," said Georgie with his tongue in the sugar bowl. "I didn't do nothin'."

Feeling nothing I watched Georgie hide the empty sugar bowl in the broom closet. I thought: I will never feel anything again. . . .

It had been a fine thrill for Hobson, Clyde and me to get the upper hand of our share of the blizzard, to bring our sheep safely home through the snarling, hounding winds, across what seemed mile after mile of unfamiliar range with the wet, stinging snow burning our faces and the terrible winds pulling the breath from us, tearing at our clothes. More than seeing our way we had had to feel it and there had been something frighteningly primitive about this. About halfway home I lost my footing for the dozenth time and went sliding downward, landing in a snow-filled hole. Two sheep had beaten me to it and the three of us threshed around quite a bit trying to find our way out. I located a rock and found by standing on it I could feel the hole's rim but I could not haul myself up. The two sheep and I might have perished there but for a moment of quiet in the tempest which allowed Hobson to hear me screaming for help. I remember my massive anxiety until I heard his voice above me, "All right, all right, I'm here. And here's Clyde. Are you hurt?"

"I don't think so. There are two sheep down here with me. There's a rock here I can stand on but—"

"Stand on the rock and give me your hand, Fern. Here I am, I'm right above you."

"What about the sheep?"

"Stand on the rock and give me your hand, Fern."

"No! The sheep first. I am going to hand them up to you head first."

"Fern, you can't. You aren't strong enough. Forget—"

"No! I am going to wrap them in my coat and when I hand them up you pull and I'll push. You ready?"

"You're crazy! Crazy! I always knew it!"

"Here is the first one. Grab him. Grab him! Pull! He isn't all that heavy."

He *was* all that heavy and so was the second one but we got them out and then with Hobson's help I got out. I thought Clyde would have a fatal, running fit before I stood on solid ground again. I thought my back might be broken from all the heaving and straining but did not dare complain to Hobson, he was so mad at me. He snatched my coat from the second rescued sheep and threw it at me. "There. Put it on."

I said, "I will in a minute. Right now I'm hot."

"Put it on! You want pneumonia?"

I put the coat on and, following Hobson's orders, Clyde and I assumed the homeward lead then with Hobson bringing up the rear. Papa didn't find us until we were within about a mile of the house. In the snow-filled wind he appeared before me like some white apparition. He shouted to me, "Where is Hobson?"

I screamed my answer. "He's back there! He's coming!" Any more conversation was impossible. For the first time in my memory Papa held out his hand to me and I put one of mine in it. When we were within vision distance of the house the storm began to abate.

Now, with feelings I could not sort out, I sat on a chair in the kitchen of our house watching Georgie hide the sugar bowl in the broom closet. My knees would not stay together, they kept sprawling sideways and I could not stop shivering. I knew I was never going to be warm again. I thought: We are not going to win here. It is going to be like all the other times. Why? WHY IS THIS? What have we done that is so wrong, that we always, *always* have to lose?

Georgie was backing out of the broom closet. He skipped to the door to open it for Hobson and Papa. Clyde was with them and he came at once to me and put his head on my knees. Hobson was a sight. Both of his eyes were swollen almost shut, the collar of his coat was hanging loose, he was filthy. Papa looked ready to drop, yet as he sat down in his chair at the head of the table he looked around at us and, as if he understood he must say something to assure us and pull us together, spoke to us with prairie simplicity. "Well, that was some blow, wasn't it?"

"Yes," said Hobson, strangely patient. "Some blow."

137

I said to Hobson, "We have a new baby sister."

"Papa told me," said Hobson. "And I know he doesn't work at the bank anymore. We've been in the barn talking."

I glanced at Georgie who had climbed up on his chair. There was sugar on the tip of his nose and in the corners of his mouth. Importantly he sat with his hands folded in his lap and some inner action touched me. Why, I thought, there is nothing mysterious about him. He is just a normal little boy. How could I ever have thought all those silly superstitious things I used to think about him? He has never lived before. This is the first time for him just like it's the first time for the rest of us.

Madge had brought two cups of coffee to the table, one for Papa and the other for Hobson, and Papa, after taking a long sip of his, said, "All right now, kids. Pow-wow time. We are going to talk but let's keep our voices down because your mother and Ruth are asleep."

"Powwow," whispered Georgie and slipped from his chair and went to stand beside Papa, crooking his neck around to stare into Papa's face with a fixed expression.

There was weak sunshine at the windows. The wind and snow had ceased; the sky was clearing.

Papa had loosened his coat and opened it but did not remove it. He began to talk to us in an exact, steady tone. There was no pity in it, it came from some deep preserved place within him. He began to draw a battle line for us, giving us himself, awakening, for the first time in our lives, his true relationship to us. Making us feel important not only to him but to ourselves. And to the world which had always seemed to hold us in such contempt.

He said, "Hobson and I were out in the barn talking just now and we've decided we should start shearing now. The man at the stable in town used to be a sheepman and every day since our car quit I've talked with him. No, he won't come out here and help us. He's old and nearly blind but he's been good enough to advise me. He says this: It is not too cold to shear if it is not too cold for ewes to lamb. And shearing should be done before lambing begins. That way you have clean udders for the lambs and you cut down on the chance of infection. Now then, I've been doing a little detective work and I'm convinced our lambing time is just around the corner so we've got to make some tall tracks. I think we'll shear in the barn but first it has to be cleaned. The sheep are tired today and want to rest. There's enough feed in the barn for them to last several days."

"Georgie and me will feed them," said Madge. "He's big enough to help with things. Aren't you, Georgie?"

Georgie nodded. "And we'll take care of Mama and Ruth too." He leaned and rubbed the sugar clinging to his face on Papa's sleeve. His crime was going to go unpunished. How sweet and safe and good the world was.

"I thought," said Papa, "I could clean the barn today. Hob, are you and Fern too tired to take the dray to town and bring back enough hay to cover its floor? It needs fresh bedding and we need some other supplies too."

"We aren't tired a bit," said Hobson, illumined. He

was sitting erect in his chair and so was I, our fatigue dissolved. Who can be tired when they've just been returned from the dead?

Papa handed Hobson several money bills. "I don't expect miracles but make this stretch as far as you can. The ox is in the ditch now."

"Ox?" said Hobson, his hand to his jaw.

"Ox?" cried Madge. "I didn't even know we had a ox. What ditch is he in?"

"Kids," said Papa. "That's just an expression. We don't have any ox in any ditch. What I mean to say is, it's either sink or swim for us now."

"I don't know how to swim," said Georgie looking at Papa as if to quell an outrageous threat to his life.

Papa took Georgie onto his lap. "I know you don't. When summer comes I'll teach you. We'll go to the creek and I'll give you lessons." He turned his attention to Hobson and Madge and me again. "You're worried about money. Yes you are, I can see it in your faces but don't be. When Mr. Kincaid fired me he gave me an extra two weeks' salary and if necessary your mother will write to her aunt in Kansas City and borrow enough money on this land and house to tide us over until we can get ourselves straightened out here."

I put my knees together and this time they did not sprawl away from each other. I heard the newest member of our family crying. *Waaaaaa, waaaaaaa.* She was speaking openly for herself as Papa was speaking openly for himself and for Mama. Through the window beyond

Papa's head I saw the sky. It was turning blue. Settled weather was in prospect.

Every ranchsteader knows you can do almost anything if you have to. When there are things you don't know how to do you find out through the mistake-and-try-again method.

Sheep should be dry at shearing time. Ours were. So was the weather. For the job we used the simplest equipment: a pair of two-dollar, hand sheep shears, a large square of clean canvas, some special string to tie the fleeces and some six-foot sacks. In the sacks the wool would go to market.

The first young ewe Papa brought from the corral to the barn for shearing did not want a haircut. Much like a child during that first terrifying trip to the barber she bawled and squirmed and put up a fight, dancing around on the canvas, jerking and kicking every time Papa approached her. We worked for what seemed an hour trying to coax her to stand still and when that did not work we tried force. You would have thought we had murder on our minds the way this one squealed and howled and threw herself around.

Finally Mama, who had come from the house to watch, left the barn and returned with a handful of new grass. She knelt on the canvas in front of the ewe and the animal took an eager step forward, sniffing. *What's this? GREEN grass? Oh, kind lady, beautiful lady. Is this really for me?* Delicately she lowered her nose into

Mama's outstretched hand and took a well-mannered nibble.

Mama spoke to her. "All we want from you is your wool. Will you stand still now and let us take it?"

The ewe rolled her eyes and smacked her lips. *Take it. I'm through with it for this year. I can grow more.* All the fight went out of her.

"See?" Mama said, smiling at Papa. "They're just like children. Remember the time we gave Georgie his first haircut? How we had to bribe him?"

Papa grinned at her and I felt a warm ripple pass through me. We all watched as he put his left hand on the ewe's head to steady it and with his right began to shear, working backward from the head to the tail, the idea being to keep the fleece all in one piece without making any waste motions. But when he had finished with the first ewe we had several greasy, ragged rugs and a painfully ugly animal with all her defects showing —old wounds, discolored splotches, little skin knobs.

Exhausted, wet to his waist with sweat, Papa released her before I remembered it was my job to brand her with a line of lanolin-based dye that would mark her as our property.

Hobson criticized me for my lack of attention to work. He carried his tirade too far and Mama said, "Oh, Hobson, she hasn't committed any crime. It isn't anything that can't be fixed. You're too much like your Grandfather Bacon and I want you to stop it. Take this young lady back to the corral and bring us another one.

North, how many pounds do you think we got from this first one?"

Papa went to the sack containing the wool which Hobson had trampled. Hefting it, he made a calculation. "I can't guess. Maybe eight pounds. I wish we had a scale. And I sure wish I knew how to shear. You see these fibers? They're too short and won't bring the price they should. Well, here's the next victim. Will somebody please bring me a big glass of water?"

Shearing is a cruel job for the tenderfoot. To prevent blistering Mama wrapped Papa's hands in strips of old, soft bed sheeting and he wore canvas work gloves but still the blisters came. Papa said, "I know there are machines made for this job and next year we're going to have one."

Our clients were not all as balky as the first had been. Some even seemed to enjoy shedding their winter clothes and pranced back to the corral in their spring outfits like Saturday night flappers.

Mama gave me the key to Colonel Harbuck's house, told me to saddle Ned and ride down there, to see if I could locate any kind of scale.

The Colonel was just back from Rapid City. When I rode into his yard and dismounted and he came out to meet me the thought went through my mind that he was certainly the spirit of something in his black Stetson hat, fine waddy boots and smartly styled riding britches. He carried a black quirt. He said the blizzard hadn't done any damage to speak of to his place. He was one of those people who know how to hang an atmosphere on every situation.

He said, "A scale? No, I don't have one of those but I'm a good judge of weight. Just give me a minute to saddle up Old Paint here and I'll ride back to your place with you. When I was a kid, before my mother and the government tried to make a gentleman out of me, I lived at Belle Fourche and used to work on a sheep ranch during my summers. That was one of the best times of my whole life. I'll bet I haven't forgotten how to shear. How do you like the looks of Old Paint? I bought him in Chokecherry yesterday."

I said, "He's handsome enough."

"Do you like his name?"

"It isn't very original."

"Well," said the Colonel, jumping on Old Paint. "Names don't mean anything to a horse." He galloped out across the prairie ahead of me. He was that kind of person who belongs in South Dakota—open-hearted, free- and true-speaking, unconventional. But his timing was wrong. He should have lived back in the wilder, less hampered days, those of the ranging buffalo and the leaping antelope.

Kill the buffalo! That's what Colonel Harbuck wanted to do. Only there weren't any left to kill. If there were they were making themselves scarce. There was only the prairie, the endless prairie, calm, empty, mystic, beginning now to show its first dressings of spring.

The Colonel was one of those men who do not favor female strivers much. Ned and I outstreaked him on the way from his house to ours and I thought this nettled him a little. When we reached our barn he jumped from his horse, ran inside, took one look at Papa and said, "Man, don't you know what a neighbor is for?"

"We didn't know you were back," apologized Papa.

"Give me those shears and send your women to the house," said Colonel Harbuck. "My Lord, you look ready to cash in."

"I am," admitted Papa.

The Colonel had removed his hat and was in the process of removing his shirt. At noon when I went out to announce dinnertime he was kneeling on the canvas working shoulder to shoulder with Papa. Both had stripped to their underwear and were having a fine time. They had Hobson jumping around, trampling the wool in the sacks and applying our paint brand to the shorn, a scarlet back stripe which would dissolve in the wool-washing process used in the commercial wool industry.

The Colonel and Papa put their clothes on to come to the house to eat their midday meal. I got up enough nerve to ask the Colonel if he had received any valentines that year and he said, "Why, yes I did. Your little sister sent me one and signed your name to it. How did I know? Well, there's a slight difference between the signature of a child and that of a young lady. Say, this corn pudding is delicious."

Webb Harbuck's eastern schooling had not spoiled him for his place in our West. His swagger and know-how fitted in with the scenery and the people. He did not drink liquor himself but on Saturday nights usually rode Old Paint into Chokecherry where he soon became known as an energetic peace negotiator between those sad, weak ones who sought solace for their loneliness in the bottle. He was a showman and eventually became sheriff of Chokecherry.

Also he was a salesman. It was he who found a buyer for our wool, a merchant in Rapid City, and negotiated by telegraph the right price for it.

Chapter Eleven

When lambing time comes the sheep raiser might just as well remove the hands from all household clocks and personal timepieces. For, whether this most important performance of the whole sheep year takes place out on the range or in lambing pens especially constructed inside barns or other farm shelters, it exacts a scope of talents undreamed and sometimes unheard of and is no respecter of day or night.

Here is how our lambing pageant went that year. Following the advice of Colonel Harbuck and aided by him, Hobson and Papa built two lambing pens, each four to five feet square, inside our barn, setting them against the east wall and leaving only several inches of space between the lower boards to prevent the new little woollies from crawling from one pen to another. The floors of these were spread with clean straw.

Colonel Harbuck told Papa, "North, we ought to have a heat lamp in case the weather turns off cold or some of the lambs come weak but I don't know about hooking it up to this wiring out here. Looks mighty decrepit to me."

"It's worse than that," admitted Papa. "It was finished before we ever got here. I know it's dangerous but we'll have to use kerosene lamps for light and if we should need heat for the lambs we'll use the kitchen. We've got two fine assistants here to do our running for us." With a jerk of his head he indicated Hobson and me.

The weather was quiet and relaxed. The rams had not been allowed to run with the rest of our flock for some time but each day had been taken out separately to feed and exercise. Sometimes they are rough with ewes.

And now we separated the older ewes from the younger, more timid ones and took these bunches out one at a time. Clyde seemed to sense what all these different maneuvers were about. If a ewe went behind a rock or disappeared into a thicket and was gone for more than five minutes he would come streaking back to me sounding the alarm. *Quick, quick, a lamb is coming!* And we would go running to locate the cud-chewing, resting ewe.

Colonel Harbuck put a lot of miles on Old Paint

during this time of waiting. He insisted on paying Mama for the meals he took with us.

I don't suppose I shall ever see again such a dramatic production as was displayed the night Albert, our first lamb, was born. At supper lightning began to flash out over the prairie and masses of clouds piled on top of clouds began to move down from the distant hills toward us. The temperature which had been warm all that day took a sudden drop and our valley began to fill with fog.

Papa said, "Much as we need it I sure hope this doesn't mean rain but I'm afraid it does. What do you think, Webb?"

"If it gets any colder I think we'd better move all the expecting ones to the barn," replied Colonel Harbuck. "The goats won't tolerate rain; we'll have to leave them inside but we can turn the horses out to give us more room. I'd hate to lose even one lamb or ewe to pneumonia."

He and Papa rose from the table and started toward the door just as Clyde's alerting bark sounded from the corral. "That dog missed his calling," remarked Colonel Harbuck. "He should have been a veterinarian." He and Papa rushed out.

Mama handed Ruth Patience to Madge and commanded Georgie to go play the piano. He said, "Play the piano! Now? No! I want to see the lambs get borned."

"Go," said Mama and he went.

The green and yellow lightning flashes crackling up

close to the house and out over the range now showed us the clouds rolling away to the east but still there was no improvement in the temperature.

Mama instructed Hobson and me to renew the flame in the stove's firebox, fill its water reservoir and set the teakettle and a deep foot basin, both filled with fresh water, on the range top to heat. She was calm as she said, "Let the dishes go, Fern. Your father and Colonel Harbuck might need your help. You and Hobson go to the barn." She took Madge and Ruth Patience into the sitting room to listen to Georgie's mad, savage recital.

Madge said to me, "I don't want to see any of it. It scares me."

Hobson and I also were scared of what we thought we might have to witness in the barn. Which was not a feeling to be ashamed of. To watch, for the first time, any farm animal give birth is enough to kink up anybody's insides for days.

Hobson and I said nothing to each other as we went across the yard and entered the barn by its side door. Papa and Colonel Harbuck were both inside one of the lambing pens kneeling beside a ewe in labor. She was having a bad time of it, heaving and puffing and straining, her lips pulled back in an awful, grinning grimace.

Something was amiss. There was some kind of interior trouble. Aware of it, the young ewe tried to get to her feet but could not. Groaning and twisting, her eyes implored Papa: *Help me. Help me.* The lights from the kerosene lamps drew ghostly shapes on the barn walls.

It had begun to rain; I could hear its drumming on the roof.

"North," said Colonel Harbuck to Papa, "this little mother needs some help. There's a leg or something else tangled up inside her I think. One of us is going to have to go in and locate the trouble. Let me see your hands."

Papa held up his hands.

"They're smaller than mine," said the Colonel. "If it's going to be you, you should go to the house and wash and disinfect first."

I heard my voice, faint and far away. "I could do it. My hands are small." But Papa was on his feet, jumping over the highest board of the pen, running for the side barn exit.

The Colonel sat back on his heels looking at Hobson and me. "This happens sometimes."

Hobson was suffering for the suffering ewe. "It's terrible, terrible. Is every one going to be like this?"

The Colonel was fussing with a tray of medicine supplies. "No, they won't all be like this. I wish we had some heat in here." He moved again to the ewe, stroking her back, trying to comfort her. "Hang on, girl, hang on. Help will be here in just a minute."

Birth, I thought. Mothers oppose their own lives to it.

The drumming on the roof had increased. At the side door of the barn Papa was yelling for Hobson to come open it and he and Mama, both with their arms shining wet to their scrubbed and disinfected elbows, came rushing in. Mama wore a clean apron over her dress but no wrap or head covering. Drops of rain made her brown hair sparkle.

Colonel Harbuck opened the hinged gate to the pen where the laboring ewe lay and Papa and Mama went in and knelt beside her.

Papa said, "Jenny, better let me do this."

Mama gave no indication that she heard. In a minute she put her hand inside the ewe and began a gentle, probing examination. There came her calm verdict. "The lamb is lodged in the canal. Something . . . Webb, some lubricant, please. Ah, there we are."

Hobson did not watch this proceeding. I did. The wind blew the barn's side door open and a rush of cold air swept in.

The lamb was coming. First its two front feet appeared and then its nose and then its whole body. It was still in Mama's hands. She said to Papa, "North, wipe the mucus from its face so it can breathe and let's get it dried off. As soon as the blood stops flowing in the cord we can cut it and tie it. There, I think it's safe to do that now."

Colonel Harbuck cut the umbilical cord off about four inches from the lamb's belly and tied it in two places and Papa painted the navel with iodine. The lamb appeared lifeless and Colonel Harbuck snatched up a piece of clean burlap from the stack beside his medicine tray, took the lamb from Mama and began to energetically rub it. Still the lamb did not move or open its eyes.

"Maybe it's dead," said Hobson.

Mama's mouth said, "No," but her eyes said, "Maybe."

Holding the lamb close to his chest the Colonel went over the top of the sheep pen and streaked for the door. Papa was right behind him and I was right behind Papa. We pounded across the wet yard and up the back steps. Georgie opened the door for us. His shriek wrecked the peace of the house. "What's the matter? Is that a lamb? Let me see. LET ME SEE! What's wrong with it?"

"Georgie," thundered Papa, "get out of our way." He gave Georgie an ungentle push.

The Colonel was at the stove testing the water in the foot basin with his elbow. It was steaming and he yelled for Papa to "Cool it, cool it! We don't want to scald this little fella. We just want to heat him up."

Papa added cold water to the hot in the basin and Colonel Harbuck lowered the lamb into it, all but its face, holding it there, swishing it around.

It is dead, I thought, and pain gripped me. I heard Madge's voice coming from the sitting room; she was singing to Ruth Patience. Colonel Harbuck's face above the steaming basin was dripping. I could not look at Papa. It was all too much to endure, too outrageous, too real, too much of a bitter mystery.

Colonel Harbuck's head was swathed in white steam. There was a sudden movement in the water in the basin and then there was the Colonel's shout of triumph and then Papa's voice saying, "Well. Well, now."

Our little troublemaker had opened its eyes. Colonel Harbuck lifted it dripping from the basin, we dried it off, wrapped it in a soft blanket and laid it, until it was thoroughly warmed, on the oven door.

Sometimes, if a ewe has had trouble producing her lamb or if she just plain doesn't want to be a mother she will refuse it. She will not let it nurse, she will not even look at it. If a friendlier lamb-mother can be found, one willing to adopt the little "bum," feed it and raise it as one of her own, then all is well but this piece of cunning does not always work.

Such was the case with our firstborn who became Albert by name and Georgie's property. Albert's mother rejected her spindly little squaller as did all the other lamb-mothers and so Albert became our house pet. At first he had to be hand-fed. We used a baby bottle with attached nipple. To keep his identification straight we painted the number 1 on his right ear and the same on his mother's. We followed this procedure with all the new lambs and their mothers.

When Albert was two weeks old Dr. Ross came out from Chokecherry and he and Papa and Colonel Harbuck docked and castrated him, docked all the other new lambs and castrated all the ram lambs except those selected for breeding. A docked lamb, one shorn of its tail, means a cleaner, more stylish animal. Castrated lambs, those whose testicles have been removed, are known as wethers. Colonel Harbuck said wethers bring better prices than rams come marketing time because as they mature they develop a better quality of rib section used for chops and roasts and grow better, plumper loins and legs.

Our little bum, Albert, took to human companionship and surroundings with clever ease. He allowed Georgie to sit in front of the stove holding him, rocking him to sleep. It was not an easy job to teach him how to drink milk and water from a pan but Georgie was a patient trainer. Soon Albert was mooching around the table at mealtimes, scratching at the door when he wanted in or out and making off to hiding places when he wanted privacy.

Sensing Albert was different from them in some privileged way the other lambs merely tolerated him when Georgie took him out to play with them though he was no slacker or whiner. He kept up with the best of them as they raced around hillocks and down rutted roads at breakneck speed, galloped down trails leading to nowhere, gamboled back, sides heaving, little tongues hanging out. Gleefully they would knock each other into tailspins but never bestowed this favor on Albert. Albert loved all the uproar and would roll and tumble in the grass, kicking his heels in the air, trying to invite playmates. His invitations went without profit until one day I saw a queer thing happen. Clyde, who had been watching the other lambs ignore Albert, decided he had had about enough of this injustice. He had been sitting beside me in the shade of a cottonwood tree but now he rose and sauntered out to where Albert, standing forsaken on a little hill, was yearningly watching the play of the others.

Clyde casually strolled up the hill, looked at Albert and Albert, not expecting anything out of the ordinary, looked back. His little fleecy face said, *I didn't do nothin'. I'm a good boy. What d'you want?*

Clyde pounced on him, Albert let out a loud squall and went down and he and Clyde rolled over and over. I noticed Clyde using his feet to fend his weight; he tossed Albert like a ball and in a minute Albert got the drift. *Wheeeeee, this is fun.* At the bottom of the hill Clyde let Albert go and Albert promptly climbed it again. Once more Clyde went up after him. Albert was jumping around like a goat and when Clyde was within swiping distance of him he let out a delighted bleat and jumped him. The other lambs had paused in their play to watch this game. One went running up the hill and tried to get in on this act but Clyde ignored him. *This is Albert's game. You don't want to play with him so I don't want to play with you.* The other lambs in the bunch with the same idea rushed the hill and received the same message. Clyde sent them flying. Every once in a while he allowed Albert to assist him in this. The play went on until all but Albert were exhausted. A giant among weaklings, victor among the fallen, he stood alone on the hill panting and puffing, waiting for somebody, anybody, to rise and challenge again. Presently one did. The challenger and Albert tussled on the hill briefly, Albert lost and went sailing himself but now it was understood he was to be accepted by the others.

Chapter Twelve

It is said of the people of this part of the West that we think the unthinkable and then go on and do it.

True.

It is the unthinkable that keeps our show out of the doldrums and in action. It is what gives purpose to our activities. This country is headquarters for the untried. Some of the old, raw, wild materials have vanished but the performance goes on and on.

There are crops which do not do well in this part of the state and we Drawns have lost, experimenting with them, and I think we will lose again and maybe again. But the curtain stays up.

When I see, all drawn up in review, the strong rippling rows of green running up and over our hills in the fluid arrangements we laid down in the spring and I see Clyde and Hobson in the blue distance driving our enlarged flock to fresh pasture then I know *our* curtain is going to stay up. We will persist. We will because we are the heritors of this land and its spirit.

I have discovered in myself a lustrous ambition to make every pod, every seed, every blade, every bud produce. Some of what we have planted is not drought resistant and so we pray for frequent rains.

It is July. In September, by arrangement with Mama's aunt, Hobson will go to Kansas City and attend a school of agriculture. I dread the time. I fear, come the moment for good-byes, I will make a fool of myself. I am afraid I will break down and blubber and run after him shrieking, "Hobbie, I love you! I never meant all those mean, ugly things I used to do and say to you. I only acted that way because I was a child and lonely too and didn't understand. I never thought you would leave us. Don't change in Kansas City. Come back to us the way you are now. I love you like you are. Truly."

Awful. To place such an intense claim now on our relationship. That should have been done long ago. Then it would have been simple. Now it is a tangle and maybe it's too late to cancel it all and take a fresh start.

I place this same kind of claim now on all those who belong to me. Not in words. In words there is still some distance and detachment but soon there will be a vacancy in our house and I think because of this there is improvement in our actions toward one another. The old feelings of desertion and aloneness have weakened between us.

Now there is a sense of repose among us and I like to think this extends, even, to Grandfather Bacon smiling down on us from his photograph in the sitting room. Papa has given him a new frame and I like to think the reason we are here is a realization of something intended.

Today our valley is saturated with sunlight.

Yo-de-lo-da-lay-tee-hee!